"I'm _____ his
is your _____ ged on

a
ja

If
sen
mas
won

But i
again
sweet
like an
day. He
her beg
a treasur

Brides for Billionaires

Meet the world's ultimate unattainable men…

Four titans of industry and power—Benjamin Carter,
Dante Mancini, Zayn Al-Ghamdi and Xander Trakas—
are in complete control of every aspect of their exclusive
world… Until one catastrophic newspaper article
forces them to take drastic action!

Now these gorgeous billionaires need one thing: willing
women on their arms and wearing their rings! Women
falling at their feet is normal, but these bachelors need
the *right* women to stand by their sides. And for that
they need billionaire matchmaker Elizabeth Young.

This is the opportunity of a lifetime for Elizabeth,
so she won't turn down the challenge of
finding just the right match for these formidable
tycoons. But Elizabeth has a secret that
could complicate things for *one* of the bachelors…

Find out what happens in:

Married for the Tycoon's Empire by Abby Green

Married for the Italian's Heir by Rachael Thomas

Married for the Sheikh's Duty by Tara Pammi

Married for the Greek's Convenience by Michelle Smart

MARRIED FOR THE SHEIKH'S DUTY

BY
TARA PAMMI

First Published in Great Britain 2016
By Mills & Boon, an imprint of HarperCollins*Publishers*
1 London Bridge Street, London, SE1 9GF

© 2016 Harlequin Books S.A.

Special thanks and acknowledgment are given to Tara Pammi for her
contribution to the Brides for Billionaires series.

ISBN: 978-0-263-91669-0

Our policy is to use papers that are natural, renewable and recyclable
products and made from wood grown in sustainable forests. The logging
and manufacturing processes conform to the legal environmental
regulations of the country of origin.

Printed and bound in Spain
by CPI, Barcelona

Tara Pammi can't remember a moment when she wasn't lost in a book—especially a romance, which was much more exciting than a mathematics textbook at school. Years later, Tara's wild imagination and love for the written word revealed what she really wanted to do. Now she pairs alpha males who think they know everything with strong women who knock that theory *and* them off their feet!

Books by Tara Pammi

Mills & Boon Modern Romance

The Sheikh's Pregnant Prisoner
The Man to Be Reckoned With
A Deal with Demakis

The Legendary Conti Brothers

The Unwanted Conti Bride
The Surpise Conti Child

Greek Tycoons Tamed

Claimed for His Duty
Bought for Her Innocence

Society Weddings

The Sicilian's Surprise Wife

A Dynasty of Sand and Scandal

The Last Prince of Dahaar
The True King of Dahaar

The Sensational Stanton Sisters

A Hint of Scandal
A Touch of Temptation

Visit the Author Profile page at
millsandboon.co.uk for more titles.

CHAPTER ONE

"WHAT ARE YOUR requirements in a bride, Sheikh Al-Ghamdi?"

Sheikh Zayn Al-Ghamdi stared unseeing at the flat-screen monitor that was attached to the wall in his office. Words came to his lips and fell away.

He had known for a while now that this final step of settling down and marrying was coming at him. It had been drilled into him since childhood that he would one day marry a woman who would serve him well as a wife and his country as sheikha.

Of course she would be mostly an image that would be carefully cultivated and supervised to please the people of his country. He had also been taught, by example of his own parents, that her role even in his life would be very minor. Having his children and continuing the legacy of the Al-Ghamdi family was going to be her primary duty.

Last week when Benjamin had invited him and two other men to confab, following the exposé in *Celebrity Spy!*, he had been the one to suggest that all his problems would be solved if he married and started producing heirs.

All three men, his rivals for years, turned reluctant allies—Benjamin Carter, Dante Mancini and Xander Trakas—had looked at him as if he'd grown two horns and a tail. Until they had seen the sense in his idea after their initial grumbling and posturing.

But faced with the question asked by Ms. Young, the billionaire matchmaker recommended by Xander, he found himself bewildered.

In the little slice of his life that he was actually the master of, Zayn resented being brought to heel like a dog by some bottom-feeding, trashy tabloid.

But thanks to the dirty exposé on the four of them, his image was utterly besmirched. His parents, even though retired from public life, still had lectured him over his image, the effect of every small minutia of his life over the political climate of Khaleej. Even worse, his sister Mirah's fiancé's family was talking about canceling the match.

Conservative to the core, they didn't believe he had a right to any kind of life, much less the kind of reckless debauchery the article hinted at. But that was not acceptable.

Ten years younger than he was, his sister had been a ray of sunshine in an otherwise solitary life. From their parents' aloof, almost cold, upbringing, to the rigors of preparing for a political life, if not for Mirah, Zayn would have known no true joy. No companionship at all.

"Sheikh Al-Ghamdi?"

"My bride needs to be attractive and young. Attractive enough for me to be able to look at her for the next five decades. And healthy enough to have children. Someone not approaching or close to thirty."

Ms. Young made scrupulous notes but Zayn saw the vertical frown between her brows. "Is there a problem, Ms. Young?"

Her gaze couldn't quite hide her judgment. "Women are known to have children even at the *advanced* age of thirty, Your Highness."

"Yes, but women reaching thirty have stubbornly decided ideas, Ms. Young. They will not be malleable. I might not meet their expectations of an ideal man, either."

The woman didn't quite snort but Zayn had a feeling she wanted to. "A woman ambitious about her career will not do. She'll have to understand that her role in life is to complement me."

"So beautiful but not really smart."

"Yes. She will have to come to me as a virgin."

Outrage flared in Ms. Young's expressive eyes. "That's barbaric."

"That's the only way I can ensure there's no future scandal or shame attached to her name."

"Virginity need not be required. We check their backgrounds very thoroughly before we make matches based on your requirements."

"Ex-boyfriends and old lovers have a way of showing up in one's life to make the most trouble. I would like to avoid any future scandals concerning my Sheikha and her past. This ensures it."

"Beautiful, young, malleable, not particularly smart and a virgin. I don't know whether to say this is the easiest or the hardest match I've ever made, Your Highness."

"Are you saying you cannot find me a woman to match those requirements, Ms. Young?"

"Of course I can, Your Highness. But I just wondered if love was going to be a part of the equation."

"You run a matchmaking business for billionaires, Ms. Young. Has love ever been part of it?"

"I was curious about your opinion."

"Some foolish, fantastic notion will not make my marriage a success. I require a wife who will yield to my superior judgment in all areas of our life and be an asset to my political life."

"A kind of accessory?"

"The perfect accessory, if you will," he finished, amused at the flicker of anger in Ms. Young's eyes.

He had known for a long time that was all a wife could be for a man like him.

Two weeks later

In all her carefully mapped-out adult life, Amalia Christensen had never imagined that one bright, hot-as-Hades day she would be waiting in the administrative offices of the ruling sheikh, Zayn Al-Ghamdi. In the spectacularly grand palace of her father's homeland, Khaleej, she stared at the breathtaking domes and ornately lavish halls decorated in pure gold.

In the time that she'd lived with her mother in Scandinavia, a lot of things had changed in Khaleej, and for the better.

With infrastructure improved to rival any western nation, and its meteoric entry into the global finance world, Khaleej was now a flawless blend of artistry, tradition and technology.

If not for the constant knot of worry in her gut about her twin, Aslam, she'd have been clicking pics and Instagramming left, right and center. The rust-colored palace with its turrets and domes, sitting in the center of hundreds of acres of landscaped gardens and a golden sandy beach corralling it on one side was a visual feast.

But in all the years that she'd yearned to visit Khaleej, she hadn't imagined doing it this desperate way. The beauty of Khaleej and her reconnection with her roots was empty, meaningless, without Aslam by her side.

If only she'd visited last year; if only she'd understood how restless and angry Aslam was…

It had taken her two months after arriving in Sintar, the

capital city of Khaleej, to get this meeting with a palace official. After one short visit with Aslam, who had poured out the entire story to her in the jail; several tense, monosyllabic conversations with her father over the phone—Amalia had no interest in addressing the decade-old silence that still stood between them—followed by endless reaching out to friends of Aslam and learning about the instigator of the whole escapade; and finally, asking her boss Massimiliano to use his connections and arrange this meeting for her.

Massi had laughed and asked if it would bring back the best executive assistant he'd ever had to work for him. Glad that he hadn't written her off during her long-term leave, she'd promised to return soon. Much as she missed her career and cringed at the dent in her savings, she couldn't leave until Aslam was free.

The sound of the glistening blue waters of the gulf gently breaking onto the pristinely white sandy beach, visible to the right of her, added a background score to the pregnant silence of the corridor.

She'd been told the palace was usually a beehive of activity. Instead a sort of hush reigned over the scarcely occupied hall.

Neither did she forget the diatribe that had flown out of the official's mouth that Amalia's appointment had been scheduled on *that particular day*.

There was hardly any staff around, either.

What was going on?

She'd never been a royalist and yet the recent exposé on the four bachelors, one of whom was Sheikh Zayn, had drawn her interest. Apparently, the sheikh led a very colorful and inventive private life away from the highly conservative media of the country and the grueling lifestyle of his powerful position.

Amalia had seen the numerous articles that had mushroomed following the exposé, questioning Sheikh Zayn's dedication toward the governing of Khaleej, the conservative ideals of most of the cabinet and his very image in the eyes of his people.

She glanced at her watch one more time and stood up from the comfortable sofa. Her thighs groaned from sitting for far too long.

Gold piping in the mosaic tiles winked at her. A quick glance behind her showed no hovering security guard, and she slipped through a grand archway into a long corridor that looked like it belonged in a fantasy novel.

A blast of heat hit her and she realized that the corridor opened into a courtyard on the left. Pristine white marble gleamed for a mile or more in front of her. In a moment of uncharacteristic impulsiveness, Amalia slipped her feet out of her pumps.

With the cold marble kissing the overheated soles of her feet and a soft breeze coming in from the bay touching her cheeks, the sheer beauty of her surroundings calmed something inside her.

In the three and a half hours since the harried-looking official had asked her to wait, if you didn't count the hour she'd spent standing at the reception, waiting for the said official to appear in the first place, Amalia had begun to see a pattern emerge. Guests were being shown into this wing of the palace with the utmost secrecy and security for there would be a sudden rise in the activity around the reception area every half hour or so.

And with each group, there had been almost always one designer-clad, elegantly coiffed woman in the center, quite like a queen bee in the center of her hive.

Guests of the sheikh?

Passing a sun-dappled courtyard dotted with cool fountains and swaying palm trees on her left, she wondered why the women were being brought to the palace.

They could be applying to join the sheikh's harem, the man having decided that he needed recreational variety closer to home now that his extracurricular activities had been exposed to the world's media.

She snorted. Not even the playboy sheikh could justify a harem in this day and age. *Could he?*

What if he was building a strip club sort of thing here in the capital city of Sintar for his personal use and they were women from all over the world at the top of their career in pole dancing? A modern-day harem for one man—wasn't that pretty much what a strip club was?

Not much of a leap, given that *Celebrity Spy!* had said the sheikh's sexual appetites were voracious…

Or they could be princesses and queens and top-tier dignitaries from all over the world attending a banquet given by the royal family—hadn't she read somewhere that his sister was to be married soon?—which meant the man who'd promised to see Amalia was probably busy with the details of the banquet and not coming for hours.

The second prospect sobered her spirits. But she couldn't leave until she spoke to him about Aslam and the bogus drug charges built up against him while the real perpetrator was hiding in the lap of luxury.

The moment the palace official had agreed to see her, Amalia knew she'd been on the right path. Someone high up had to know they weren't Aslam's drugs.

She glanced behind her to the archway and realized she'd walked quite a way.

A heated conversation in the courtyard to her left lifted the hair on her neck. Alarmed, she opened the first door on her right and slipped inside.

Walking in from the bright light of the day momentarily

blinded her vision. Faltering on her feet, she reached out with her hands and found a wall.

It took her a few seconds of blinking and focusing before she could see around the room. Her stomach quivered.

The room wasn't completely dark as she'd thought first. A large skylight at the far side of the vast room cast a golden glow, showing a man sitting on a throne-like chair, complete with dark gold upholstery and clawlike feet. As if he was the king of everything he surveyed.

Shivers spewed over her spine, as if there was a predator in the room.

Light brown eyes first flicked to the pumps in her hand and then to her bare feet. "You are carrying your shoes instead of wearing them. Why?"

With a jerk, Amalia dropped the pumps and with them, *plop* went her heart.

Unlike the staff that had catered to her, the man spoke English with an aristocratic, upper-class accent. A deep baritone made the words fall over her like drops of ice-cold water over heated skin.

Without looking at him directly, she could feel the man's intense gaze on her mouth. Her lips quivered. "I…I walked out into the courtyard and I was too hot."

"I see that you are too hot." The dry statement jerked her gaze up. Intelligent and imperious, his brown eyes were wide-spaced and hooded under the dark slashes of his eyebrows. And brimming with amusement. "Why did you walk into the courtyard?"

That made her tongue come unstuck from the roof of her mouth. "I got tired of waiting. If I had to sit on my behind any longer, I'm sure it would have been flattened under me, that's how long—"

"I hope our furniture didn't cause your…posterior any lasting *harm*."

Her hand went to the particular section of her anatomy. "It's hard enough to find clothes that fit my height within a budget, so yeah, a flattened backside is not good. And nope, it's perfectly fine," she quipped. And only after she spoke the words did she realize this whole line of conversation was ridiculous.

Embarrassment sent heat flooding up her neck, blocked her throat. And she wished she had a genie in hand, like in her father's elaborate stories, to make herself disappear. Or at least, start over this whole conversation.

"I didn't mean to interrupt…"

"Apology not required," he said, and Amalia bit down on the retort that she hadn't been offering one. "The process is taking longer than it should." A hint of irritation peeked through that sentence. From anyone else, it could have been an apology. But Amalia was pretty sure he didn't intend it to be one.

She pushed her feet into the pumps. One hand went to her stomach as if to shoo away the butterflies rioting in there, and one went to her hair. She expelled a sigh of relief when she realized her tight ponytail had stayed put. Once she made sure all of her person was intact—she needed that assurance—she raised her gaze.

Between one rushing heartbeat and the next, she became aware that the man's utter dominance, over everything in the room, even over the very air she was struggling to breathe, was bred into his bones. His power clung to his skin, not his clothes or to this room or the throne.

It was centuries of legacy, she realized, a sheen of sweat covering her forehead now. He looked like a king because *he was a bloody king*. Or to use the right terminology, His Royal Highness, Sheikh Zayn Al-Ghamdi of Khaleej. Brilliant statesman, inventive playboy that *Celebrity Spy!* claimed liked fast cars, fast technology and fast women.

Her first instinct was to mumble an apology and run from the room. The element of surprise was on her side and if she just went back through the unending corridor, back to the waiting area, she could lose herself and slither out of the palace.

Poised on the balls of her feet, Amalia forced herself to calm down and reconsider.

This was the sheikh, *the man with all the power*, the man who was responsible—*fine, indirectly*—for Aslam being wrongfully imprisoned. What were the chances that she would ever get an audience with him again?

No way could she tuck her tail between her legs and run away just because the man had to be the most dominating presence she'd ever felt.

Her breath seesawed through her chest as he stood up from the recliner, prowled the width of the room and then stood, leaning against an immense white oak desk. A sitting area to the right had a chaise longue.

Although *lounging* seemed like too still an activity for him.

The energy of the man, his sheer presence, filled the room and pressed at her from all sides, as if to demand acknowledgement and acquiescence.

A shining silver tea set on the side table made her aware of her parched throat.

As if she'd voiced her request out loud, he moved to the silver service, poured a drink—mint and lemon sherbet—into a tall silver tumbler and walked over to her.

That sense of being overwhelmingly pressed on a sensory level amplified. He had a sandalwood scent. And he gave off heat like there was a furnace inside him. Or was that she who was feeling the heat when really he was giving off none?

Sensations she didn't like and couldn't control continued to pour through her and Amalia just stood there, shuddering inwardly in the wake of them.

Where was the super-stalwart Amalia that Massi depended on? Where was the woman who'd been dubbed "the calm in the storm" by colleagues and coworkers?

"Drink. Strangers to the country forget that even when they do not sweat, the heat is still unrelenting."

His command was supercilious, arrogant, exaggeratedly patient. Better if he thought her brain had short-circuited because of the heat than because of the sheer masculinity of the man.

"I'm not a stranger."

His gaze swept over her. "You do not look like a woman from my country."

She took the tumbler and drank the sherbet without pause. The liquid was a cool, refreshing breeze against her throat. Even her head felt better. Lowering the glass from her mouth, Amalia wondered if the man's theory had credit.

Really, she'd been meandering for almost twenty minutes. Was it a stretch that she had lost her composure because of the heat? Armed with that defense, she extended the glass back to him. "Thanks, I needed that."

He didn't move. He didn't take the glass she offered. He didn't speak, either.

Slowly, Amalia raised her gaze and looked at him. Really looked at what had to be the most aggressively masculine specimen on the planet.

And promptly realized all her theories about heat and dehydration messing with her composure were just those: theories with a hefty dose of self-delusion.

Tall windows above and behind her cast just the right amount of golden light onto his face as if they, too, had been beat into submission by the will of this man.

A single brow rose imperiously, his gaze very much on her face. A gesture filled with a dark sarcasm. Was it because she had given the glass back to him, as if he was a servant? Was his sense of consequence so big that he was insulted by her innocent gesture?

He had short, thick, curving eyelashes that shaded his expression—a tactic she was sure he used to intimidate people. Light turned the brown of his eyes into a hundred golden hues, the eyes of a predatory cat.

Square jaw, rough with bristles, sat below high cheekbones and a straight nose that lent his features a hardness she didn't like. His mouth was wide and thin-lipped. A mouth given to passion; the strange thought sent a shiver down her spine.

Amalia was tall, only two inches short of six feet. He topped over her easily by four or five inches. His neck was the same glistening tone as his face—a dark golden, as if he had been cast from one of those ancient metals that Khaleejians had used several centuries ago. Her father had had a small knife whose handle gleamed like his skin tone.

He propped a finger under her chin and lifted it up. All of her being seemed to concentrate on that small patch of skin. "Your appraisal is very thorough after being so flustered."

Heat poured through Amalia's cheeks. "I wasn't flustered."

"No?" The brow-rise again. "A lot of women lose their composure when they see me."

"Second of all," she continued, "you look like a man who needs to be met square in the eye, Your Highness."

Amusement filtered through the implacability in his eyes. "That is a bold statement to make. Tell me your name."

"Ms. Christensen."

"Did your parents not give you a first name?"

She didn't want to tell him her name, which was the weirdest thing Amalia had ever felt.

He waited and the silence grew. "Amalia Christensen. I was dehydrated. Now I've found my bearings again."

Taking the coward's way, Amalia stepped back from the sheer presence of the man and made a meandering path through the room.

A haunting memory of listening to one of her father's stories of ancient history of Khaleej gripped her. A traditionally designed curved dagger, almost the size of her lower arm, hung against a beige-colored rug on the wall, its metallic hilt gleaming in the afternoon light. She ran reverent fingers over the handle.

Yet, she couldn't leave the infuriating presence of the man behind. It was like trying to ignore a lion that was sitting two feet away from you and eyeing you for his next meal. Neither could she curb the rising panic that the longer she took to explain herself, the harder it was going to be to convince him to help Aslam.

The scent and heat of him rubbed up against her senses.

"This is a fifteenth-century *khanjar*, isn't it?" she said, just to puncture the building tension around them. "Men used to wear them on their belts. It was a sign of status, a sign of prowess."

"Among other things, yes," he said drily, and a fresh wave of warmth washed over her.

"A sign of their macho-ness, in modern words," she added, tongue-in-cheek.

It seemed they didn't even have to look at each other for that almost tangible quality to build up around them. Was it just awareness of each other? Attraction? Or was it her fear of the consequences of her pretense that was making her heart ratchet in her chest so violently?

"Decorative pieces now."

His surprised gaze rested on her face but Amalia looked straight ahead. She couldn't rid herself of the lingering sensation in her gut.

"You've studied the history of Khaleej in preparation for this interview?" he said, a thread of something in his tone. "I have to admit to both surprise and admiration for that. Having a knowledge of Khaleej and its customs is a huge point in your favor."

Interview? For a position with him?

For the first time in two months, luck was on her side. If it was a job among the palace staff, a position closer to the sheikh himself, much better. Maybe she wouldn't have to blurt out the truth this minute and risk getting on the wrong side of the man.

Would waiting only make it worse for Aslam? Which option was better?

"Yet, I didn't receive a file on you from Ms. Young."

Face coloring, Amalia pulled her phone out of her bag. "I can email you my résumé in a minute."

"No, that is far too…*strange*, even for me."

Now, what did he mean by that?

"Tell me about yourself. I'm curious why Ms. Young picked you to be a candidate when it's clear you don't have a royal connection or any other advantages."

Royal connection? How high up was this job that there were candidates with royal connections applying?

"I didn't actually prep for the interview," she said, deciding to dole out truth little by little and see how he reacted. She needed to get a sense of what kind of man he was—if he was fair-minded or just like his cousin.

"I was born here in Khaleej and lived here until I was thirteen. My…father is a historian at the Sintar University and an expert on antique objects. He…" The sudden lump in her throat made it hard. "My twin, Aslam, and I…it used to be our favorite pastime to sit in his study and listen to his long, rambling stories about Khaleej. He is, or used to be, a consummate storyteller." So good that she'd utterly believed him when he had said he'd send for her very soon. That had been more than a decade ago.

"Used to be?"

"I haven't seen him in a while."

"You seek to make a home in Sintar again, to reconnect with him?"

"No. And I have no intention to." He frowned and she added, "No intention to reconnect with him, I mean. I have other reasons for being here."

"But you do not have a Khaleejian name."

She shrugged. "My mother and he divorced and they split us up. She took her name back and asked me if I wanted to, as well. I said yes."

"You should have your father's name. You should have something that speaks to that part of your heritage."

"I don't really see why when he and I have had nothing to do with each other," Amalia retorted, angry with him, angry with herself for reacting at all. She was supposed to learn about his temperament, not pour out her own nonexistent relationship with her father.

His frown sliced through her anger. "My point is I would be an asset in any position with my understanding of the cultural norms. My Arabic is rusty but I can polish that up, too."

He gave her one of those considering looks again. Never had she struggled so much to hold a man's gaze. "That is good but might not be completely necessary. Both parts of your heritage could be put to use. You could be the western connection that Khaleej needs."

So it was a position in close quarters with him? Excitement and alarm twisted in her stomach.

"Tell me more about yourself, Ms. Christensen," he invited in a languorous voice.

Keeping her gaze on some point left of his face, she began, "I worked for five years as an executive assistant to the CEO of a multimillion-dollar company. I'm fluent in four languages. I never lose my cool." The raised brow again, damn it. "And I work extremely well under pressure. Also, I'm very good at managing public relations and media, too."

"You sound like a paragon of hard work and efficiency, Ms. Christensen."

"You sound like it's a bad thing," she retorted.

He smiled, and Amalia for the first time understood the meaning of *knee-buckling*. Her fingers tingled to trace the grooves in his cheeks.

"I should warn you that this is unlike any job you've worked at before. What are your expectations?"

"That I would be compensated well and dealt with fairly."

He laughed then. She'd been right. Full of his own consequence he was, but he also had a sense of humor. The laugh lines around his mouth sat easily on the hard contours of his face. "Your bluntness is refreshing. You know that monetarily, you will be set up very well for the rest of your life." He sobered up. "As to being treated fairly, I always treat women well."

"Have I convinced you that I am right for this position, then?"

"I'm holding judgment on that. As you know," a glint in his eyes made Amalia aware of her own skin, the rapid beat of her heart, the slow tingling low in her belly, "it is not a decision I can make in a half hour. But you will be glad to know, on paper, I would have rejected you immediately. I have to hand it to Ms. Young. She made a bold but different choice with you."

"You would've rejected me? When I'm supremely qualified?"

"Defiant as you are in rejecting your Khaleejian heritage, I can't believe you can be that naive about your suitability, Ms. Christensen. Khaleej is at the most troubling and exciting point in history now, straddling ancient traditions and the modern world. Everyone around me reflects on me."

Amalia prided herself on the career she'd worked so hard for. She'd dedicated years to it, had looked after her mom before she'd passed away last year, paid for her endless treatment... His dismissal of her stung. "Just tell me why," she demanded.

"A career woman full of her own ideas about independence and gender equality and with a grudge against her own father is the last thing I need on my hands."

All those fluttery, useless sensations that she was beginning to recognize died a sudden, much-appreciated death as Amalia tried to wrap her head around the sheikh's statement.

If he didn't want a professional, dedicated, experienced career woman for the position, how did he expect to get anything done? What use would a woman who couldn't think for herself be in—?

Her heart sank to the soles of her sensible pumps.

It wasn't a job he was interviewing for.

And if it was a stripper or a belly dancer she'd insanely thought, well, he'd have asked questions about that field, wouldn't he? Maybe even asked her to give a trial performance. But even that crazy idea was better.

Her pulse skidding everywhere, her eyes wide, Amalia stood rooted to the spot as the last piece of the puzzle slotted into place.

That was why the palace was mostly empty, why women had been brought in all morning. The Ms. Young he kept mentioning wasn't a headhunter but a matchmaker.

Sheikh Zayn Al-Ghamdi of Khaleej was interviewing eligible candidates for a wife, for his sheikha, and Amalia Christensen, dedicated career woman and valuer of her independence, had inadvertently applied for the position.

Her pulse skittered as fear filled her veins.

What if she had ruined Aslam's only chances for release with her dangerous charade?

CHAPTER TWO

AMALIA CHRISTENSEN WAS the kind of woman who made men grateful for being men, who brought forth all the uncivilized, rampantly aggressive instincts that men pretended they didn't feel anymore to cater to the modern feminist's sensibilities.

He had never been struck by an attraction so hard and so fast.

The way she'd been so hotly flustered when he'd let his gaze sweep over her lithe form had been incredibly interesting and stroked his masculinity in a way he hadn't needed in more than a decade.

Zayn couldn't turn his gaze away from the color seeping up her cheeks or the way her expressive eyes flashed her dismay, confusion, followed by the resolve. He could practically see her spine lock into place.

Khaleej had always been a progressive nation. Even Zayn agreed there was a place and reason for gender equality and the feminist movement.

Just not in his life. Or in his bed. He had no doubt that he, in particular, would be deemed a *male chauvinist* or an *antifeminist devil* for there was no room for another strong personality in his life, let it be a lover or a wife.

He liked and preferred women who understood and accepted that he was the dominant one in bed, that he would take care of all their needs as long as they trusted him. As long as they were equally wild as he was.

Every aspect of his life had been controlled, first by his father and then by himself, and would continue to be until he was dead. But his private life, his sex life—it was where the wildness in him ran free.

With the little time he had, contrary to the *Celebrity Spy!* lurid exposé about his alleged orgies and depraved tastes, he needed his sex life to be easy and simple, not an ongoing battle of sexes.

So Amalia Christensen—with her long, wavy, dirty-blond hair tightly pulled back in a ponytail that brought her exquisite features into stunning focus, her pillowy, lush mouth that argued that she wasn't flustered when she so obviously was and her hot little body hidden in her buttoned pencil skirt and long-sleeved top—was not the kind of woman Zayn would engage with sexually.

If she was the innocent type who couldn't even own her sexuality, he didn't have the time or patience to teach her. If that innocence was a cunning act to attract his attention, he didn't want to play that game.

Neither was her vehemence that her father's heritage had no part in her life something he liked. Clearly, she had been raised to disrespect authority figures, encouraged in her rejection of an important part of her identity. He would bet her mother, who had given her those light brown eyes and the stunning golden-blond hair, was the author of that disillusionment, too.

So Ms. Christensen was not fit to be his wife in any form or way.

Was this Ms. Young's rebellion because he had ruffled her sensibilities with his requirements in a wife? She couldn't have believed Zayn would choose this contradiction of a woman to be his sheikha in a hundred years.

But after a morning of meeting eligible candidates— all lovely virginal women with connections in high places and with a full understanding of what it meant to be the future Sheikha Al-Ghamdi, docile and respectful of his country's norms and traditions, *and* even more important, thoroughly and admittedly bowled over by what he represented—this woman was a maddening, arousing novelty. His response to her and her rough, almost insulting manner was both curious and irrational.

Because staring into those long-lashed, honey-colored eyes, he couldn't help wishing he'd met her a few months ago. Even a month ago, before the episode of *Celebrity Spy!* and ruffled sensibilities of his countrymen.

She was nothing like the women he slept with but she completely intrigued him—a novelty—and that would have made the chase and the final victory that much more exciting.

For a minute he wondered if he could give her a position in the palace and keep her close. Until he was married and Mirah was happily married and the dust settled around his image. Until he was free to pursue her... No. Even for a man who considered marriage nothing but an advantageous step in his preordered life, the idea was utterly distasteful.

He had long been resigned to the idea that, like his father, after a few years of marriage, he would find sexual satisfaction with other women. But beginning his marriage with a mistress in mind was repugnant.

He should be sending her on her way. He should think back to the women he had met this morning, make a decision and get it over with. Move on to the next task in his unending list of state duties.

"Have I insulted you by that statement, Amalia?" he said instead, using her given name on purpose.

Just as he expected, her mouth tightened. Her shoulders went back into a ramrod line, which thrust her breasts out provocatively. He had a feeling she'd never do that if she knew how alluring that gesture looked.

"I'm wondering why you're not sending me on my way if I'm such a bad candidate, Your Highness. I'm also wondering how to make the best of this situation. It seems my options are lose-lose."

Something in her eyes, a conflict, a hesitation, made him think she wasn't just sparring with him anymore. She was upset by the sure outcome of this meeting and she was mustering defenses.

Had she been so sure that she would impress him? Would this alliance mean so much to her?

Or had she conspired with Ms. Young to lure him into an alliance of a different nature? Why not? Women tried to attract his attention in every which way. He was known to be a kind and generous lover. If there was a connection he could use in high places, or a recommendation he could make to advance the current woman in his life's career in some way, he'd always been open to it.

Was this Amalia's game? Had she somehow inveigled this invite so that she could present herself as a candidate, but for something altogether different?

Doubts ensnared him.

He didn't forget that even though she'd lost her footing, she'd recovered her composure very well. She had been the most interesting woman he had met today among all the candidates. The most interesting woman he had met in a while, if truth be told. But was that interest being cultivated and engineered with a purpose in mind?

"In your life, are there any skeletons I should know of?"

Instantly, her gaze shuttered; a paleness touched her skin. Guilt was a shining emblem on her forehead. He'd been right. The woman was here under false pretenses and convoluted motives.

Send her away, one voice inside his head said.

Play her at her own game, another said.

"You're hiding something. Or are you counting your lovers in your head?" something savage and out of control goaded him to ask.

Outrage filled her eyes. "That's none of your business. Unless you're offering to do the same count for my benefit. Will you reveal what you ask of me? Should I pull out the *Celebrity Spy!* exposé and tally your number against theirs to verify the veracity of your claim, Sheikh?"

Utter scorn, for him as a man and for his position, reverberated in her defiant question.

Instead of being infuriated, Zayn smiled. He deserved that after his probing remark. Still, he found himself unwilling to give up this sparring match with her. With every back and forth, he knew he was indulging himself in something that was fundamentally against his principles. Against the little personal respect he had put aside for his wife's position.

But the compulsion was fierce, the urge too primal to be denied. There was something about her that called to things he'd never before experienced. "It is my business if we are going to consider this, Amalia. And I will not apologize for having lovers in the past."

He hadn't decided on a candidate yet. Technically, he was still a single man. Even if that line was very thin right now. He ran the tip of his finger over her cheek. Her skin was gossamer silk under his hands. "Every past and present aspect of your life is going to be considered fair game. There has been enough scandal in my life and I do not want to deal with jealous ex-lovers."

She didn't push his hand away. A fine tension began

to vibrate from her. "That's a double standard, and you know it."

Why didn't the infuriating woman just tell him about her past? What was this curiosity that drove him to learn about a woman he could have nothing to do with? "The world is full of them."

Chin tilted at a defiant angle, she stared back at him. "So let me get this straight. If I have my hymen intact, it will give me a few more points on this list of yours?"

The fire in her eyes, the soft tremble of her lips...it made Zayn think of sultry nights and damp, tangled limbs.

"I will tell you my expectations, then. You will be given a certain amount of freedom. Your primary role will be to present an image of a healthy marriage and to give birth to our children. An affair with another man will have disastrous consequences. The media will rip us into shreds and the country will be in uproar."

"Is Your Highness promising the same fidelity in marriage, then?"

It was already a fantasy, this game they were playing with each other. This pretense they were both playing at, knowing that it was leading nowhere. Only one thing they both wanted.

She had to know that he would never marry her. He had told her that. And yet, she was still here, provoking him, luring him in for a taste. An affair with him—was that truly what she wanted, then?

Even in the charade, Zayn wouldn't lie. "On the contrary, I fully expect that within a few years, the reality of our marriage and the pressures of this life will make us, if not hateful, at least indifferent toward each other. And when that day comes, I intend to seek another woman. I'm sure you'll be glad to not have to bear my unwanted attentions. I enjoy sex and I do not intend to give it up."

"And this is your idea of marriage? This is what you've been offering all the women you've been meeting all morning?"

"No. All those women already understood these terms and accepted them. They knew even before they saw me today, that that was reality. It is only for you I see the need to set the expectation."

"Because you think I'm naive enough to believe in love? To believe that a man like you will offer fidelity and respect and love?"

The cynical light in her eyes shocked him. Why, when she was clearly here with not so pure motives... "No, I explained it all because I thought it would tell you that I'm as unsuitable a husband for you as you are a wife for me. Marriage to each other would be war, Amalia, and I have enough of them to contend with in the other areas of my life."

"Wait, you thought I'd be heartbroken that you're rejecting me for the role of your wife and this is you softening up the loss for me?"

"Yes." Before she could skitter away from him in her outrage, Zayn cupped her neck and arrested her movement. The small indent at the base of her nape was the sexiest part of a woman he had ever touched.

He swallowed his shock at how swiftly lust rose through him.

Her breath fell in rough exhales while a tight stiffness entered her body. He held her loosely enough to not threaten her, leaving it in her hands if she wanted to move away. Other hand sliding to her waist, he exerted enough pressure to bring her closer to him.

Gorgeous brown eyes widened into innocent pools. Very likely, the vulnerability in her eyes was a well-rehearsed act, but still it turned him on incredibly. Pursuing one sophisticated woman after the other, sleeping with women who knew the score, Zayn had forgotten, or maybe he had never known, how hot this kind of vulnerability was.

He wanted to kiss her. He wanted to make her all flustered again. He wanted to see if she would taste sweet as her soft sigh said or tart as her words suggested. When it came to women, Zayn had always taken what he wanted, pursued models and actresses ruthlessly. He wasn't going to let this rough-around-the-edges woman slip past him.

"I'm going to kiss you, Amalia. This is your moment to go all outraged on me and call me a savage beast."

If possible, she stiffened even more in his hold. "I… refuse to provide you with any more entertainment. I was right in thinking that you would be just as bloated and corrupt with power as—"

Whatever outrage Amalia had amassed to fight the man's autocratic ideas and her own out-of-control senses, all of it disappeared as Zayn's mouth touched hers.

The scent and taste of him was an overwhelming assault on her senses. He tasted of mint and some dark potency that stirred everything in her to waking. Heat poured through her in rivulets as he pressed one tender kiss after the other, from one corner of her mouth to the other. The softness of his mouth—who could know such a hard man could have such soft lips?—was a delicious contrast against the rough scrape of his jaw, tugging Amalia's senses this way and that.

If he had kissed her with the aggressiveness she sensed within him, or if he had employed that sensual mastery that had made him a favorite lover of women, maybe she would've resisted.

But instead the soft flick of his tongue against the seam

of her lips, the kisses punctured by the sweetest endearments in Arabic, Amalia melted like an ice cube on a hot and sultry Khaleej summer day. He tasted her as if he was dying to probe all her beguiling secrets; he kissed her as if she were a treasure he had just discovered.

This supposed connoisseur of women requested entry into her mouth as if she was the most enchanting woman he had ever met. And sensible, rational, rarely discomposed Amalia fell for it all. She eagerly opened her mouth under his questing one.

And just like that, the tenor of the kiss changed. It went from a pleasant seaside breeze to an intense scorching heat wave. His tongue swiped over the moist recesses of her mouth, teasing and taunting her tongue to play with him. The stroke of his tongue over hers released a dampness between her thighs. It was what he had done with words, too. He had somehow provoked her, called the part of her that she didn't even know existed, made her revel in the moment, made her prolong what was only a dangerous charade.

He was seducing her mind.

He was doing that now, too. It was as if he knew to soften his aggressiveness for her, to slowly draw her out instead of demand. At least until she came to him of her own volition.

With a shamefully wanton moan, she sank her fingers into his hair and pushed herself closer to him. She sucked his tongue into her mouth just as he had done with her.

Large hands roved over her body now, tracing the ridges of her shoulders, the line of her spine, setting every nerve ending on fire. Urgent and aggressive, he stroked every inch of her to the same need. Amalia had never felt like this before and she didn't know how to stop it, how to gain control over herself or this madness that had overtaken her.

All she knew was that she never wanted to stop.

Her mouth stung and her nipples peaked to tight points, grazed again and again by the hard contours of his chest. His hungry hands finally stilled on her waist and he pulled her even closer. Mouth left hers, giving her a chance to breathe. "Point proven. You can huff and puff and act outraged but truly, you want me. And you can't see how all your self-control and rules about needing respect and recognition before attraction are out the window already. That's what all this feminist bluster is about, isn't it?

"It's not about my double standards but about your own conflict in wanting me when you do not want to."

If he had slapped her, Amalia couldn't have been more shocked. It was like being drenched in an ice bath to douse her overheated senses. Still, her body throbbed in all these newly aware places, slow to cool down.

With a disgusted growl, she pushed away from him and turned around. Lungs burned as if she had run a long distance, her mind blank under the onslaught of such heady pleasure.

She rubbed her palm roughly against her stinging lips as if she could get rid of his taste. A horrified sound escaped her mouth. Dear God, she couldn't believe she'd been kissing the Sheikh of Khaleej.

The thought of her twin rotting in that jail cell while she played ridiculous games with the man who held his fate in his hand made nausea whirl up through her throat. How could she have forgotten Aslam so thoroughly?

How had she gone from asking for help to a harmless pretense to climbing all over him like a vine?

"You're offended by the kiss. But I will not apologize for doing something both of us wanted."

She whirled around, his self-assured words scraping at

her. Could she blame him for thinking she was putty in his hands? "I'm not just offended. I'm disgusted with myself."

He laughed again. And this time the sound was redolent with mockery. "Because you got what you came for? Or because you enjoyed the kiss thoroughly?"

"What I came for?"

"You and I both know that you're not suitable to be my wife in any way or form. So the only conclusion I draw from your being here is that you came seeking an affair. It is not a secret, *anymore*, that I treat my women well."

The gall of the man to think she had expressly come so that she could lure him into an affair. Was there anything bigger in the world than the man's ego? "You mean you pay them for sex?" she hurled at him.

His mouth curled, a hardness entering his eyes. "I do not like games, Ms. Christensen. I do not find affected outrage of the kind you're displaying attractive at all. If you find my conclusion that offensive, why don't you tell me why you're here?"

This was it, her opening. To prolong hiding the truth meant resigning Aslam's life to the jail cell for who knew how long. And yet, Amalia hesitated.

Something in the glittering gaze, in the sensual but hard contours of his mouth, told her he wasn't going to like it. He wasn't going to forgive her easily and then offer to help with Aslam. She might have made it worse if the sheikh thought she'd made a fool of him.

She was completely screwed.

"I did not come here hoping to marry you. In fact, I don't think there's a couple in the entire world more unsuited to each other for marriage."

His hands behind his back, he looked at her as if she was one of his subjects. "My sentiments exactly. So I see only one reason why you would be on Ms. Young's list."

"No…I'm not one of the candidates lined up for your pleasure by Ms. Young. I would never allow myself to be presented like prize cattle for viewing."

His hardened jaw told Amalia she was only making it worse, but she couldn't stop. "I figured that much, too. Which is why I have to believe that you came here seeking a different kind of alliance."

"I'm not here for an affair with you."

"No?"

"A hundred times no. I came to meet with a state official about my brother Aslam's case. I have spent two months dragging myself from one state office to the other, hoping someone would listen to me. He is in jail for—"

"Ah…so you're a family of criminals, then?" His eyes were cold, flinty, his mouth a study in utter distaste. "Brother goes to jail, and sister inveigles herself into the palace under false pretenses. Is your father really a historian? Is anything you told me the truth?"

Amalia flinched. Her credibility was zero with him and she had no one but herself to blame. She softened her tone, hoping it would appeal to his good side. If he had one. "All I did was tell a white lie. No, I didn't even do that. I just didn't clear it up. I…couldn't pass up the opportunity—"

"Opportunity to do what? To get into the sheikh's chamber? To present yourself as a temptation?"

He looked so threatening right then, Amalia could practically feel the power coming off him. Utterly different from the man who had kissed her so tenderly, even from the man who'd laughed so openly. "Of course not! I don't want to kiss you much less want an affair with you. I have a successful career and do not need any favors from a man like you, whether given freely or in exchange for something else."

She now realized how fooled she'd been by the *Celeb-*

rity Spy! Article, too. Having read about the sheikh's escapades and orgy fests, she'd decided in her head that he
was someone she could persuade and plead with.

But the man who stared at her with those inscrutably
brilliant eyes didn't have a soft bone in his body. The last
thing he looked like right now was a self-indulgent, reckless playboy the exposé had called him.

"I intended nothing like that. I was tired of waiting and
I snuck in here out of pure panic. When I realized who you
were, for a few minutes, I even completely forgot..." She
flicked her eyes closed for a second. Not everything had
to be revealed now, even if he knew what her reaction had
been to him. Opening her eyes, she willed her tone to be
matter-of-fact. "Aslam has been imprisoned unfairly for
something he was only a marginal part of. He was angry
at life and reckless and irresponsible."

"How old are you, Ms. Christensen?"

Amalia couldn't figure out what he was getting at.
"That's neither here nor there."

"I can have your entire history in my hands in ten minutes."

Domineering ass! "Twenty-six, Your Highness."

"It's a little late to be all deferential, yes?" He folded
his hands and leaned against the table. The crossing of
his ankles stretched the black trousers tight against the
length of his thighs, and Amalia had to force herself to
pull her gaze up.

When was her body going to move past the fact that the
man was insanely, knee-meltingly gorgeous and a domineering, arrogant tyrant who thought every woman was
out to ensnare him?

"So your brother is, too. You know what I was doing at
that age, Ms. Christensen?"

Partying with your groupies, she wanted to say, but she held her tongue.

He smiled then, as if he was perfectly aware that she was biting down on her tongue. Hard. "For three decades, there have been constant skirmishes between Khaleej and our neighboring country. I was at a weeklong summit, working nights and days to sign a peace treaty that would end useless bloodshed. Once the treaty was signed, I partied, hard. Your brother is not a teenager. He has to face the consequences of his actions."

"He doesn't deserve to spend the next decade in jail when the actual perpetrator—"

"What is your twin in jail for?"

How she wished she could offer a different answer, to stop the guilty flush from climbing up her neck… "Possession of illegal substances, with intent to sell."

Instant judgment pursed his mouth tight. Her heart sank. "There's nothing I can do about it. Sentences for drug possession and distribution are meant to be harsh. He shouldn't have been using if he doesn't have the constitution for jail. And really, to send his sister to—"

Amalia covered his mouth with her hand, rage burning through her. And yet, seeing her white knuckles against his golden skin sent a shock through her, too. As did the warmth of his mouth searing through her palm. "I didn't come here to sell myself just to save my brother."

Long fingers gripped her wrist and pushed her away. "No?"

"I came hoping that your administration was a fair one. Even after I saw you and realized what you thought, I kept quiet because I thought you would be fair like you promised."

Tears threatened and Amalia pushed them back. No way was she going to cry in front of the callous man. He was picking his own damn wife from a marriage mart, like he was picking an outfit for the next week. The minute she'd realized that, she should've known he was going to have no sympathy for her case. It was clear Sheikh Zayn Al-Ghamdi had no heart. "I should've known when I spoke to your cousin that you'd be no better than him.

"Aslam is serving the sentence for what your cousin did. He took that package from him because he couldn't refuse someone 'so cool,' in his words, and yes, because my brother is a reckless, foolish idiot who didn't know who he was trusting. Your government is bloated with corruption and no wonder *Celebrity Spy!* exposed the truth of you like that.

"I wouldn't be surprised if the entire Al-Ghamdi family is a bunch of corrupt, drug-trafficking, womanizing men bloated with power."

CHAPTER THREE

"THAT IS ENOUGH, Ms. Christensen," Zayn retorted in a tone that would brook no more nonsense. "It is my family, the royal house of Al-Ghamdi that you speak of."

"And you're above law, is that it?"

"My family has its share of hangers-on and lazy fools, Ms. Christensen, like anyone else's," he added drily and had the satisfaction of seeing her flush.

He had always thought his cousin fell into that category.

A harmless one though...

No one in his entire life had spoken to Zayn like that. Even when he was learning to walk, he'd been the prince, the royal highness. Mirah had been born ten years later and though he shared an affectionate relationship with her, she'd never challenged him or provoked him.

Growing up, and even after he'd gone to university, Zayn had never really had a confidant. No one who had the guts to call him on his ego, or arrogance or his sense of importance.

Even his rivals, Xander, Benjamin and Dante, who were probably the only people on the planet who weren't intimidated by his title and all it entailed, still addressed him as Sheikh.

Infuriated as he was, he couldn't help notice one thing.

Ms. Christensen believed her brother to be innocent.

And her loyalty to said foolish, imbecile brother seemed to be absolute.

Being dedicated to his own sister's happiness, it was a trait Zayn had to admire in the woman, if nothing else.

Since his temper was dangerously close to tipping over, which was a rarity in itself, he decided he needed a breather from her. And from the annoyingly lingering taste of her.

Now that he was thinking rationally again, he realized there had been a certain lack of experience in her kiss. Dare he think that annoying innocence, that vulnerability in her glazed eyes as she looked up at him, was real?

His mind wanted to wander in too many distracting and interesting directions and Zayn curbed the urge.

A suitable wife who would fix his image in the people's eyes, that was what he needed, not a conniving waif on a wrongfully guided rescue mission.

His gaze resting on her thoughtfully, he picked up the phone on the desk. In minutes, security would guard both the entrances to the office. He didn't trust her to not escape or bamboozle some other unsuspecting man into helping her.

"You will stay in this room until I return, Ms. Christensen. If you try to leave, the guards will manhandle you to stop you and then you will cry brutality at the sheikh's hands. I would like to really not add anything more to the headache you're already causing me." Truly, his head was beginning to pound in earnest.

Damn it, he should have never kissed her. He could not show even a small weakness, could not let her have any power in the strange dynamic between them.

The woman seemed extremely resourceful when it came to cunning.

To lose his head and kiss her was one thing. But to have

not believed his own instincts that something was odd about her from the beginning, bordered on foolishness. Foolishness that could cost him another scandal that his image couldn't risk and worse, Mirah's happiness.

She sprang toward him with a jerk. Lilacs, that was what she smelled of. Zayn took a deep breath before he could restrain the foolishly indulgent impulse. "Wait, you're imprisoning me here and leaving?"

Deep satisfaction filled him at the panic in her eyes. Finally, another way to fluster Ms. Self-Sufficiency. "Nothing so dramatic, Ms. Christensen. I need to go deal capital punishment to the state official who kept you waiting and the guards who should have caught you before you snuck into my private office. Maybe I'll fire the entire incompetent staff. In the meantime, I didn't want you to escape. I still haven't decided how I'm going to punish you."

Her skin became a deathly white, her hands wringing each other. She blocked his path, her slender body radiating tension. "Capital punishment? That's barbaric. They probably were busy escorting the contingent of women you ordered to be brought here, back and forth. You probably can't see past your bloated ego but this palace is a maze and I'm sure they can't be everywhere at once and…"

Her chest fell and rose, drawing his attention to her high, deliciously full breasts molded under the soft cotton T-shirt. Her scarf that she had used to wrap loosely around her neck and upper body was trailing from her left arm, exposing what she'd been hiding all this time. Narrow waist that he could probably span with one hand gave way to full hips that made her prim pencil skirt into something altogether provocative. Tall and yet curved, the woman had a model's figure.

He waited, enjoying the gloriously outraged picture she presented.

"You tricked me!" she said in a voice full of outrage. "You purposely made me believe those men would be punished for something I did."

He laughed, surprised at finding humor in the whole farce. "You're not the only one with tricks up their sleeve, Ms. Christensen. Now stay put until I come back."

It took him twenty minutes, fifteen minutes too long in his opinion, to surmise the situation.

One of the staff members who knew someone in the legal department had scheduled a meeting with Ms. Christensen. When Zayn had questioned how the woman, a stranger to Khaleej, had known to not only contact the said official but also to arrange for a meeting with him to obtain her brother's release, his personnel had all frozen in terror.

Finally, the shaking man had come forward and said that the request for meeting had come from someone higher up in the department. Specifically on the recommendation of a Massimiliano Ricci.

It seemed at least that part of her story was true.

Zayn vaguely remembered meeting the Italian businessman, known for his cutthroat business tactics. That Amalia had gained a meeting through him did not surprise Zayn in the least.

Was she his girlfriend, then? Didn't the man know what a menace the woman was to herself? Because if she were Zayn's, he wouldn't have let her roam Sintar alone for two months, even if she had been born here.

Nor would he have let her dog the steps of the unsavory crowd that her brother seemed to keep company with. What was her father thinking?

The next thing had been to have someone find him the case file on her twin brother. Which had taken a wasted ten minutes, which he couldn't really blame on his staff.

Lost in the beguiling scent of the blasted woman, he had forgotten to ask what her brother's last name was.

Finally, he had her brother's file and a staff member finding the identity of her father. The part about her father was true, too. Professor Hadid was very well known and respected in his circle.

Drug Possession. Intent to Sell. Waiting to be sentenced.

It wouldn't be anything less than seven years, Zayn knew. He'd been one of the members on the committee who had asked for harsher sentences on drug trafficking in Khaleej.

When Zayn had tried to reach his cousin, however, he had been informed by his aunt in a vaguely roundabout way that he was out of the country. Which really didn't tell Zayn much. His cousin Karim had never amounted to any good for all his life, but could he have let an innocent man take the fall for one of his activities? It was another headache he did not need right now.

Armed with a vague sense of discontent, Zayn returned to his office.

Amalia—he couldn't refer to her as Ms. Christensen now that he knew how potent the taste of her mouth was—was standing at one of the tinted windows, looking out into the courtyard. The fading sunlight of the evening drew a provocative outline of her body.

Her shoulders were in a stiff line, her entire stance one of defense and alertness. Despite his preoccupations, Zayn couldn't stop his gaze from running down her back this time. She was fully covered up, even though that custom had more or less been banned from being required in the last decade.

And yet the flare of her hips, the curve of her bottom, made the pencil skirt the most provocative thing he had ever seen on a woman.

He had met more beautiful women, more charming ones, women who knew how to be seductive and yet feminine at once.

She was none of those things and yet he hadn't lost his mind over a woman like this in a…actually, never. He did not like anything random in his carefully controlled life and he didn't like this strange reaction to her, either.

It made his voice harsh as he said, "I have looked at your brother's file and I have spoken to the official you were supposed to meet."

She turned around. Her hands wrapped around her midriff, under her breasts, unconsciously pushing them up. "And?"

Zayn forced himself to focus on the anxiety that pinched her features. "The evidence against him is pretty tight. And this is not the first time your brother has been in trouble with the law."

"I know. But they were petty things."

"Defaming public property, heading a strike at the university, unruly behavior in a mall…it seems like he was building his repertoire since he was fourteen. I even spoke to the detective who put together this particular case and he assured me that he was thorough."

"I never said the evidence against Aslam wasn't damning. I spent two months talking to everyone connected with that arrest. I…dogged every official who was connected with it in the lightest way. Aslam took a package from your cousin minutes before the police showed up. Which, apparently, your cousin knew of."

"You talk as if you were there."

"I believe my brother. And my research was thorough. I tracked down the third friend and then fourth. Their accounts of the incident were not the same but definitely suspicious. They seemed to want to help Aslam but when

I asked them to come forward, they became slippery."
Frustration made her voice hard. "It's obvious that they
are afraid of your cousin's connections."

"Did you not think once if it would be unsafe to find and
accost these men? What is your father doing in all this?"

"He is busy with his career and his family, not that I
asked him for help. When I did ask him to talk to someone
in the palace, he told me he believed in the justice system.
And I took acquaintances with me every time I went into
new places of the city and never at night.

"I'm independent, Sheikh, not foolish. You, like a lot
of other members of your sex, seem to equate the two."

"Give me the names of these men."

She nodded, glad that finally she was getting somewhere. "If you tell me when you find them, I can persuade
them to speak out maybe. They seemed receptive to my—"

"You will stay out of this investigation and will not continue it anymore, either."

"I can help."

"Even though your accusations have no basis, I will
check with my cousin. But he is right now out of the country and there's nothing more I can do about this for the
moment."

"Can't you command him to return? You're the sheikh,
aren't you?"

Zayn threw the file on the desk and walked toward her.
"On the word of a woman who has told me nothing but
lies since I laid eyes on her? Who insists on insulting not
only me and my title and my position, but even my government and my judgment?"

Every inch of her rose to attention at his compelling
stance. "You're not being fair. My behavior toward you
should not affect Aslam's case. Not if you were truly intent on seeing justice carried out."

"That is true. But my hands are tied right now. Return to your job, or your country or wherever it is you came from. There is nothing more you can do for your brother."

"I'm willing to apologize for my deception, if that would assuage the dent to your ego."

"You offer to apologize in the same sentence as you insult me again. And there is no dent to my ego, Amalia. You are a nuisance in a very busy schedule. And now I will stop you from being one."

"You're forcing me, Your Highness."

"Into what?" He frowned, not liking the determined glint in her eyes. "I'm making it easy on you. Despite my misgivings, I gave you what you asked for. Once he returns, I will talk to my cousin, although it might be several months."

"But Aslam would have spent even more time in jail for something he didn't do," she repeated, her voice rising. Something like a growl escaped her mouth, and slowly, her breaths returned to calm. "Fine, so be it.

"But if I walk out of here, I'm going straight to the media. To a particularly nasty tabloid paper that is already very fond of you."

"And what is it you think you can offer the tabloid? How it felt to have kissed me? Will you join the ranks of my groupies, in your words? Will you tell them you tried to seduce the sheikh and failed?"

She went pale. Zayn didn't feel an ounce of regret. She was veering from nuisance to a bother now.

"No, I will tell them why I found the palace so particularly empty. I will tell them about your Ms. Young and her list of candidates.

"I will paint a very descriptive, colorful picture of what was going on here. That I saw women being brought to the palace, to be looked over by you and to be interviewed by you.

"And maybe, I will conveniently forget to mention the fact that there was a fiancé mart going on over here." She scrunched her face up, as if this was all a joke. "I don't know. I can't decide if it looks bad if I omit the fact and let them jump to all kinds of conclusions like I did or if it is worse that you are picking a wife from a list of eligible candidates."

"What conclusions did your devious mind jump to?"

"That you were building your own personal harem."

Zayn hadn't been shocked in a while, if ever. There were very few surprises in life for him. One extremely unpleasant one had been the exposé by *Celebrity Spy!* and the domino-like disasters it had started toppling in his life.

This was the second time. Of all the things in the world, the slender, pale woman to threaten him... His anger came slowly even then, like a discordant note underneath the shock coursing through him. Slowly, that shock dissipated, too, and he was thinking rationally again.

Only one course of action was suddenly visible to him.

The woman looked like an angel—all innocent outrage and yet, she had the guts to go up against him for her brother. There was no doubt. Zayn had never met a woman like her before.

"What you're saying constitutes blackmail. And the man you're blackmailing is the Sheikh of Khaleej, the most powerful man in the country. If you tangle with me, even your lofty connections in high places cannot protect you from the consequences. I could whisper a word and ruin your career prospects forever, if you do really have a career. I could make sure your father is never employed again by any university in Khaleej."

Her skin took on a pale cast, making her topaz eyes gleam like rare gems even more. "If I'm going down, I'll take you with me. But I will not let my brother rot in jail while there is still something I could do about it. I will not leave him to your tender, inconsistent mercies."

Zayn couldn't take the risk of this woman being out in the world, armed with the knowledge she had in her grip now.

He had made a bluff and she had called him on it. And at the end of it all, Mirah's wedding would be at stake, her future happiness at stake.

And there was only one way he could see out of this. He didn't like the decision one bit. He would have to put his plans on hold for a while. He would have to make do with this stubborn, irreverent, brassy woman, at least until things calmed down. Maybe even until Mirah's wedding took place and the furor about his image and his allegedly scandalous private life calmed down.

The woman had the balls to blackmail a sheikh. While she was still thoroughly unsuitable to be his mistress, much less his sheikha, she was at least equipped to carry out this pretense; she would survive in the fierce political wranglings of the palace.

"There is only one solution I see for the situation you have created, Amalia."

"Oh, I'm Amalia again?"

Now that he had come to a decision, her adversarial tone amused Zayn. He didn't trust the cunning minx one bit but he had to admit she was an entertaining diversion after the recent publicity fiasco. "Seeing that we are going to be closely involved over the next few months, maybe even years, it seems only appropriate that I call you Amalia." He took her stiff hands in his and pressed a kiss to the back of one hand. Her hand was cold and smooth against his lips, the tremor in her fingers going a long way to smooth his ire.

She jerked her hand back as if burned. Her feet stumbled

in her anxiety to get away from him and he caught her by the waist. A sudden, raw image of that indent of her waist bared naked to him came with such forceful mastery that he loosened his hold on her.

The rough rush of her breath only heightened his awareness of her, the soft but unyielding femininity in his hands. "Now who's talking crazy, Your Highness?"

"I have to insist you call me Zayn. Or else it is going to look very suspicious. Whatever our differences in private, Amalia, we have to put on a good show for the public and the media. The chemistry I feel between us should help with that."

This time she pushed away from him again, and took several steps more. He laughed and she glared at him. "And I insist that you tell me what the hell is going on in your twisted mind right now."

He made a clucking sound with his tongue. "And here I thought your intelligence might become an insurmountable barrier in our relationship."

"What relationship? And for God's sake, if you're calling me stupid, then just do it in plain words."

"Noted for future. I am telling you that I have made my choice. You are going to be my future wife for—"

She pulled her wrap around her like a weapon and headed for the door. If Zayn wasn't blocking the door, he had a feeling she would have disappeared like the morning mist against a rising sun. If it stopped there, Zayn would have gladly let her go.

But he knew, as surely as the fact that he was taking a huge risk with her, she would not simply give up on her brother because she was attracted to the sheikh. At least, keeping her close, he could mitigate the risk she presented to his plans.

"Like hell I am."

"We will have to clean up your language, *ya habibiti*. Or no one will believe that it is a love match."

"I'm not your dear or darling. You think the world is foolish enough to assume Sheikh Zayn Al-Ghamdi is capable of falling in love?"

"I like that you're able to understand me so well already. Since it will be impossible to convince anyone that marrying you is advantageous to me in any way, we have to resort to the instant-love, must-marry approach."

She came toward him then. The anxiety and panic in her eyes went a long way toward pacifying Zayn. "I cannot marry you."

"I'm not offering the option to you." He let his upper lip curl in distaste. "I stand by my word. You're thoroughly unsuitable to be my wife. But you have very cunningly made yourself into a liability for me. A liability I have to take care of, at all costs.

"If I let you loose in the world, I have no idea what that tart mouth of yours will do. If I keep you, a strange, unmarried female in the palace, there will be talk about it. So, this is the only solution that is acceptable.

"You will be my fiancée, for all intents and purposes, until I say otherwise. And you will do so with grace and sophistication, and you will do the Al-Ghamdi family and Khaleej proud. When I deem it wise to release you on the world again, you will leave Sintar and Khaleej."

"I refuse to participate in this charade."

"The other option is to imprison you, too. Maybe I can have a special cell built for you by your twin's side. Believe me, Amalia, that idea fills me with immense pleasure."

"That's blackmail."

"Quid pro quo."

"I...no one will believe that you chose me. I might choke before the first week is up. And how do you know

I won't still go to the media, that I will trust you to do the right thing?"

"You won't jeopardize his chances of release." He still could not believe that his cousin would let an innocent man take the fall like this. "I know how strong the need to ensure your sibling's happiness could be, especially if you are the stronger one."

"Aslam is not weak. He…just, he never recovered from our parents' split."

"You were just as young."

"I learned to manage."

He laughed again. *"Can respond with calm and reason in extreme situations,"* he said, mimicking her earlier tone. "Think of it as a challenge in your job."

"Fine, but only if you promise that you will look into Aslam's matter. And not after months or years, but immediately. Order your cousin home. Have my brother put in a minimum-care facility."

His face hardened. "If he is guilty, Amalia, I warn you now, nothing you do will make me help him."

"I know that he is not guilty."

Stubbornness could have been defined with this woman in mind. "Fine. I will look into it. But remember, one toe out of line in public or in front of anyone else, one small glimpse of that irreverent attitude toward me in front of anyone else, and I will make sure Aslam never sees sunlight again.

"No one should suspect that this is a farce that came about because you had the gall to blackmail the sheikh."

Eyes wide in her expressive face, she nodded. Irritated beyond measure, Zayn left the office. Before he was tempted to either kiss or kill the woman.

Neither impulse was one he could give in to, at least in the near future.

CHAPTER FOUR

"His Royal Highness Sheikh Zayn Al-Ghamdi commands your presence for dinner in his private garden…"

Amalia barely swallowed her gasp as the guard delivered his message with a straight face and left her standing in the sitting lounge of the suite she'd been shown to two evenings ago.

She hadn't been allowed to go back to her hotel to collect her things. No, she'd been marched straight here, to this wing of the palace, and her things had been brought to her so quickly that she'd barely even missed them.

And then she'd been left to stew in her doubts and anxiety for two whole days, while guards stood outside her suite. Finally, forty-eight hours later, he was deigning to see her.

Commands, not requests…not even invites… No, *commands*. How she wished to throw the sheikh's imperious command in his face and march out of the palace and straight out of Khaleej. How had she let herself be embroiled in such a crazy scheme that was worthy of… *Aslam*?

No, not even Aslam, she was sure, would have resorted to blackmailing the sheikh, of all men in the world. A twisting knot in her stomach gave her pause.

No, this crazy, out-of-control impulsive behavior was more like her mother. Every time Amalia had brought up the issue of her visiting Aslam in Khaleej, her mother had gone into one of her tantrums.

To give in to that urge and kiss him like that, to tangle recklessly with a man like the sheikh even in the most harmless way, this was a side of herself she'd never known.

Not her. Never trustworthy, reliable, calm in the storm Amalia.

But given that she'd learned what a hard man the sheikh was, she had taken the best option available to her, even though blackmail firmly put her on the other side of the law. If she had walked out at that moment, not that he'd been willing to let her go, she had no doubt that he wouldn't have wasted another minute on her or Aslam's case.

When it came to being his fiancée, she decided, looking through her meager collection of clothes, it was best to take a pragmatic, Amalia-esque approach to that, too. She would consider it the most difficult job she'd ever worked and he the most aggravating boss ever. That would define the boundaries, put all the checks in line. She had never put a toe out of line with a colleague or a boss ever, and if she thought of the sheikh that way, too, she'd be able to keep a professional distance.

She'd never done anything to jeopardize her career. Even when there had been a chance to build something. This had to be the same.

A professional fiancée, yep, that was what she had to be. Give a good grade performance and expect a raise. Well, in this case, a release.

Feeling a little more in control of herself, she did a few squats and lunges to get blood flowing. Being cooped up inside, even if she was being treated like a special guest, didn't suit her.

She finished her shower and dressed in another long-sleeved, navy blue Henley top and a long skirt, wrapped a thick colorful scarf she had bought in one of the street markets around her neck and chest and touched her mouth with lip gloss. Since the dark blue top and black pencil skirt made her look far too monochromatic, she pulled out the gold-plated jangling bracelets that Massi had given her for Christmas and wore them on her right hand. Her gold-plated watch went perfectly well with the bracelets.

A consummate professional with just a little personal flair, she felt sufficiently armored.

The welcoming table as she entered her suite with a gold-tinted tissue box, a hairbrush with a detailed design on the frame and a gleaming bronze hand mirror that looked like it was at least a hundred years old, had hit Amalia with a sudden bout of nostalgia.

It was an old Khaleej custom. A memory of her mother maintaining a table like that in her bedroom for years after they had left Khaleej came rushing at Amalia. Any doubts she had faced the last two days about contacting her father and telling him her whereabouts cleared away. Her mother had grieved over him and her love for so long, never being whole again.

And he hadn't even asked after her since Amalia had been here.

Hardening her heart, Amalia walked out into the corridor. Instantly, the guard followed her.

They walked away from the main palace and the administrative wing, through an open courtyard and a tiled path amidst a beautifully manicured garden. And with each step they took away from the palace, Amalia saw the shift in the architecture, the subtle differences even in the surroundings.

The abode they came to finally seemed to spring out of the ground.

There were no pretentious gold-plated carvings, or

heavy, outdated pieces of furniture here. It was as if she walked from an older Sintar to a new Sintar.

Now, as the guard led her toward where the sheikh waited, Amalia felt that same feeling again. Stained glass and arches, the typical elements of Khaleejian architecture, were all there but used with a modern, almost whimsical touch.

As if the architect had wanted to free himself from the constraints of tradition and yet found himself integrating them in his design anyway. What it ended up being was a flawless blend of tradition and modernity, married by impeccable design and taste.

They rounded a bend and came toward a huge, beautiful aqua-blue tiled indoor swimming pool, the bottom of which was a mosaic tile pattern that looked like a Persian rug. Moroccan-style lamps dotted the perimeter of the pool.

With a sense of wonder, Amalia realized the pool was the heart of this building, or the home.

The inner courtyard was surrounded by richly carved wood on multiple levels and hanging plants. There were cozy nooks and crannies everywhere, with built-in seating areas comfortably accessorized with pillows, carpets and planters.

The blues of the water and the greens of the plants created a beautiful slice of paradise, a private paradise, she realized with a sudden dismay.

This was the sheikh's personal space. The contrast between the hard man she'd met the other day and the cozy atmosphere of this space, made it difficult to marry the two. But she'd be willing to bet that she was the only woman who had ever been allowed in here.

The guard slipped away.

It took all of her determination to see Aslam released

to put one foot in front of the other and continue toward where the man himself waited.

He was wearing a full-sleeved, collarless shirt in a rich brown, which made his skin gleam like burnished gold. Dark blue jeans hugged his lean hips in an entirely too sexy way. Dressed down like that, he should have passed for an average man, an approachable man. But as she had already realized, the clothes or his position didn't make the man.

On the contrary, the simple clothes only accentuated the power radiating from him. Seeing him after two days, in which she had concocted a hundred different theories, all of which reduced the potent masculinity of the man to a thousandth degree, Amalia felt a fresh surge of amazement at her own daring. She must have been truly crazy to have tangled with this man and to have kissed him, to have pressed her body against the rock-hard contours of his...

He looked up and their eyes met.

Her gaze went straight to his mouth, her mind instantly supplying the taste and heat of his kiss. He had a soft mouth, the lower lip skating between hardness and passion. Both aspects controlled his life, Amalia decided with a perceptive leap.

Wasn't that what had shocked Khaleej and the world over? That the sheikh, who was supposed to rule his political life and his administration with ruthless control had such a wild, uninhibited, almost salacious private life.

Why had he kissed her like that? The question was beating a little drum inside her head. Had it been a case of proving a point, like he'd said? Or because she'd been conveniently present and men like that couldn't resist?

One kiss that lasted maybe a few minutes and she already felt as if he owned a little part of her. As though all he needed to do was look at her and she'd be reduced to a mass of sensations and feelings.

The way her lips were trembling, she knew he was looking at her mouth. And remembering the kiss, too.

Forcing herself to raise her gaze to his, she willed her body to cool down. There was not simply desire in his gaze, if it was present at all.

No, there was something more. A calculating assessment, as if he was taking her measure again. Of course, the man didn't lose his head over one kiss, like she'd been doing for two days. He probably hadn't even given her a thought considering what a busy man he was. For him, it had been a power play in that moment, a tactic to bring her into line. And she'd fallen into that kiss as if it was a lifeline.

Hands fisted by her sides, she didn't know how long she waited like that, staring at him across the pool that separated them.

"If you are thinking of jumping in the pool to cool down, I warn you, the water is very cold."

She looked to the calm blue surface jealously. "You have an indoor pool and it's not heated?"

He shrugged, raising those powerful shoulders. "This wing is not connected to any power line. It runs on a solar generator. The pool is not heated because I like a cool dip at the end of a hot day."

The wet gleam of his raven-dark hair told Amalia he'd done just that. Suddenly, the images of his leanly honed body stroking through the blue water, powerful thighs eating away the laps, made heat flush through her.

A drop of sweat ran down her back. The intense appraisal from his eyes, the hard glint of amusement, she wished she could make her gaze inscrutable as he did. "No air-conditioning? It must be hot as a furnace in the summer, then."

"The house was designed to take full advantage of the

prevailing winds in Sintar, which flow from the north and the west, to keep the air stream circulating throughout the entire house most of the year. That and the pool together, I do not miss air-conditioning."

"And if you do, it's a short walk to the palace you own. It's not like you don't have options."

He smiled, showing his teeth. The man even had perfect teeth. "Yes, something like that. What do you think of the house? You're my first official guest. Well, other than Mirah."

Instantly, an image of a gorgeous, golden-skinned beauty coiled tight around Amalia's throat. "Mirah?"

"My sister. But she prefers all the amenities and little luxuries that electricity provides so she was not impressed. She complains that her hair gets frizzy without a hair straightener every time I ask her to sleep here."

Amalia smiled, liking the sound of his sister. Good to know there was someone who wasn't bowled over by everything the sheikh did. Well, other than her. Most of the time, at least. "It's gorgeous, so light and airy. Nothing like I've ever seen in Khaleej, and yet, taking advantage of all its natural elements."

Something in his satisfied smile made Amalia look around the house again. He knew far too much about a house. Granted, he could be one of those particularly odd and grumpy sort of billionaires who needed everything just so and constantly micromanaged the people who worked for him. "Who's the architect?"

By this time, Amalia had walked around the pool. She stopped a couple of feet from him, still not prepared for that overwhelming awareness of him to flood her. He cocked his head, as if her question had taken him by surprise. "I designed the house."

Her mouth dropped open. But she'd known at some instinctive level. There was contentment, a sort of joy in him here. "You studied architecture?"

"And international finance."

"That's...*wow*. This open plan, and not using electricity, it seems you still have the Bedouin inside you."

Shock flared in his eyes. "I keep forgetting, encouraged by your looks and your attitude of course, that you're half Arab. Maybe it is the Bedouin inside me. I can't stand being walled up so much that you lose touch with nature."

"You clearly have good taste, Sheikh." She filled her words with exaggerated disbelief and had the reward of seeing him chuckle. "Have you designed anything else? You're also obviously very talented if my humble opinion amounts to anything."

A shadow flitted across his face, wiping the easy smile away. "I have no time for it. Even seeing this project to completion took me five years."

"Then why did you study it when you knew you wouldn't have time?"

"That is a very practical question, Amalia."

"I'm a very practical woman, notwithstanding my behavior the evening that I met you. But then I was desperate and it called for desperate measures."

"Now you sound just like my father." That hardness she'd sensed in him was in full force when he spoke of his father. Amalia wondered if he was aware of it. Probably not, for he seemed like a man who didn't betray himself— whether anger or any other vulnerability at all.

"You must have always known what your future was going to be."

"Since I could fathom the world around me, yes. But I have always been interested in architecture. Sintar has some extraordinary buildings, so full of stories and anecdotes. So I made a deal with my father. If he let me study architecture along with finance, I would not grumble about my duties and be a good sheikh to the people."

Amalia forced herself to smile when he glanced at her but she heard the thread of melancholy in his voice. From the moment she'd seen him, she had only seen what the world saw. A man born to extraordinary riches and incredible power, a man who enjoyed everything it entailed, and yet, that he had studied architecture knowing he would never be able to actually pursue his dream seemed like a very hard fact to digest.

A complete contradiction to the ruthless man who had cheerfully threatened to imprison her alongside her brother. Amalia wished she hadn't asked about the house. Wished she could somehow blind and mute herself and her senses to seeing him as anything but.

"Well, you have a very good career alternative to fall back on if you fail at this one." She didn't dare look into his eyes. "It seems like that exposé did a number on your... what do they call it, your job performance rating among your cabinet and your countrymen, yes? It's a sad fact of having such a public career, I guess."

The amusement in his eyes didn't hide the level look he sent her way. "*My* people, *my* country, Amalia?"

"Yes," she said without hesitating. "This has not been my home for a long time."

"And yet, here you are, fighting tooth and nail for your brother's release. How many times have you seen him in the last decade?"

"That is neither here nor there. All that matters is he needs my help."

He poured mint tea from a silver *dallah* and Amalia took a hasty sip. Refusing to look at him, she walked ahead. "What are we eating?"

"Lamb stew, chicken kebabs and wild pulao, with *bread pudding* for dessert."

Her mouth watering at the mention of an old favorite, she whirled around. "Oh, please God, don't tell me you're a fantastic cook, too, Sheikh?"

He stood before her, as if he was aware of her trick to keep a distance between them. "No, the chef just delivered it. What about you?"

"What about me?"

He took her elbow and guided her toward one of those comfortably cozy nooks. The press of her thigh against his sent her heart slamming in her rib cage. "You have a habit of getting defensive every time I ask you a personal question." He waited till she settled onto the knee-high seating and then lowered his wide frame right next to her. When Amalia tried to move to her right, he stilled her with his mouth at her ear. "Makes one wonder what big, dirty secret you're hiding."

She made the mistake of tipping her chin up, forgetting that he was right next to her. This close, she could see the golden flecks in his pupils, breathe in the scent of sandalwood that drifted from his freshly shaved cheeks. "I'm not hiding anything," she said in a croaky whisper. "I just don't think my life's been that interesting, say, compared to an illustrious person like you."

"And yet, I think you're an interesting contradiction at best."

His voice was even more potent than his words, the deep, velvety tone pulling her in. "At the worst?" she goaded him, desperate to break the spell.

"A cunning criminal, with the face of an angel," he said. He smiled when she glared at him. "You did ask."

He spread a napkin on her lap since clearly she was

acting like she was incapable of doing anything else for herself. "Eat."

Amalia picked up her fork and dutifully forked some wild pilaf into her mouth. The richly flavored rice and the nuts and raisins in it restored her balance. Without further prompting from him, she dug into the lamb. It was succulent and only then she realized how hungry she was.

A strained silence descended as they both concentrated on the delicious food. When she had finished the last morsel, she wiped her mouth and leaned back in her seat with a contented sigh.

He did the same. His gaze persistent on hers, Amalia was forced to meet it. "If I eat like that every day," she said, searching for something, anything, even if it was inane chatter, "I will need a new wardrobe."

"Speaking of wardrobes—" his gaze did a quick sweep over her body "—how many black pencil skirts and plain, long-sleeved T-shirts do you own?"

"As many as it takes to present a professional picture," she said, annoyed beyond measure. Did he have to find fault with everything related to her?

"I have a feeling you're not dressed so primly just because you were visiting your father's conservative homeland after over a decade. I think you always dress like this—all buttoned up and neatly covered away."

Amalia got up from the seat. Looking up at her from his sprawling position, he still didn't seem to be at a disadvantage. He looked like a pasha surveying gifts brought to him and disapproving them. Blasted man! "How is my wardrobe—?"

"You will choose a new one, of course." She stood there while he finished his drink. The open collar of his shirt showed a glimpse of golden-hued skin, stretched tight over lean muscles. She had a feeling her throat was always going to feel parched around him. "A stylist will meet you tomorrow. Take my advice, and let her dress you. We're going to be celebrating our engagement, not hiding from the world. My fiancée will have to be stylish, sophisticated. Not a woman who flaunts her femininity, nor one who hides it."

"I don't hide anything. I…"

In answer, he sent his gaze sweeping over her in such a thorough appraisal that every inch of her skin tingled.

"I'm dressed perfectly enough to be your fiancée or anyone else's."

"But I'm not any man. No one will believe that I would fall for a woman like you…"

"That's the second time you've said that. And I disagree. Maybe there should be a difference between the type of women you…bedded all these years and your adorable fiancée, yes? Maybe it is my rough edges that made me irresistible to your jaded palate?"

"It won't be your tart tongue. How sensually you kiss when your words are anything but." He handed out that little tidbit as if it were a survey he was filling out while even the memory of it scorched her. "Now, tell me, are there any skeletons in your closet I should know about?"

"Is Aslam a skeleton?" she quipped.

He didn't smile. "Jealous ex-lovers? Ex-fiancés? Broken-hearted boyfriends who might decide to make a sudden appearance?"

"That's none of your business."

"You will become the focus of a media frenzy within hours of appearing with me, Amalia. Either you tell me what I need to know or my advisers will find out. And believe me, reading about your current lover's unsavory past or nefarious motives is unpalatable in the extreme."

"You have the women you sleep with investigated?"

"Not if there is nothing to hide. My reputation, this charade we're beginning, is not a joke. I will not let you risk it."

"Is there anything left to besmirch?"

"What about Massimiliano Ricci?"

Amalia gritted her teeth to swallow her ire. "What about Massi?"

"You call him Massi?"

"I call him whatever the hell I want, Sheikh. My work, my life, they are not yours to dissect or to dictate."

"From now on, they are." Arrogance dripped from every pore. "That he placed such a call for you using his connections even after two months of not working says something about your relationship."

Jumping to conclusions about her seemed to be a habit of his. Or maybe that was what he did to women who didn't jump to do his bidding immediately.

The passing thought made Amalia's spine stiffer. She wished she could tell a convincing lie, wished she could feed the hateful man what he was asking for. But she had always been honest to a fault. The little white lie she had told him two days ago had to be the biggest lie she had ever told in her entire life.

"You will not understand our relationship with each other. And I will not deign to put a label on it for you." Maybe she wasn't good at telling lies, but she was getting good at hiding the truth. Some instinct inside her refused to answer what the infuriating man was asking, refused to admit that she'd never felt anything for Massi even when she'd wanted to.

His fingers loosened around her arm, thick lashes falling to hide his expression. "All I need to know is if he will create any sort of problem over the next few months, especially when he hears of our engagement."

Months in close quarters with the sheikh—battling wits with him and with her own willpower... Her heart sank to the soles of her feet. Massi's reaction to all this was the least of her worries. "Few months?"

"As long as it takes for Mirah's wedding to happen."

She frowned. "You're doing all this for your sister?"

"Yes."

"Why? What does your fiancée have to do with her wedding?"

"Her fiancé's family is very conservative. They did not like the lurid details that *Celebrity Spy!* made up about my love life. My mother heard talk of them canceling the wedding because they do not want to be connected to a family like mine."

Amalia would've enjoyed the pressure he was feeling if it didn't directly relate to her own fate. "So they dared to cut off an alliance with the ruling sheikh?"

"Her fiancé's family is old money. They care more about perception than they do about the truth."

"Then maybe Mirah is better off not marrying into such a family."

His smile dug grooves in his cheeks. "I would think the same if I didn't know that Farid's heart is true. He loves Mirah unconditionally."

"Your father has to have some power over all this, right? Why couldn't he persuade them that Mirah is not at fault for your escapades? It's not some kind of genetic defect that she might have."

"If it were up to my father, he would cut off the alliance completely. He thinks this...matter of Mirah's love is causing far too much inconvenience to me."

"Because a son ranks higher than a daughter?" she said bitterly.

"No, a sheikh's duty ranks much higher than love." The

setting sun played shadows on his face, making him look harsher. "Love has no place in any of our lives."

"But you're going to all these lengths for her?"

"Yes, because I want Mirah to have this happiness. My life should not adversely affect hers."

"I don't understand this." He called her a contradiction and here he was. His eyes softened every time he talked about his sister. "You were looking over women that this mysterious Ms. Young sent you as if you were picking up vegetables at a bazaar. And yet, you want your sister to marry for love? Something does not add up."

"My sister's life and mine are different, Amalia. They always have been."

"So all this was damage control."

"I intended to marry, yes. The exposé brought the time forward, is all. All jokes aside, you will dress the part of my fiancée. I have a two-week trip to Europe, which should work very well for our first public appearance together. You will look besotted and beautiful and convince the world that you're absolutely in love with me."

"That might be a tall order now that I know what a hard-ass you are."

"Then remember the fervor with which you were moaning when we kissed. If you want a repeat, I'm happy to oblige."

"Why can't we just announce to her family that we're engaged? Why does all this have to take months?"

"We will let ourselves be seen together. The ring on your finger and your adoring looks should prove to the world that I've fallen for your charms."

Suddenly, he produced a sheaf of documents from somewhere. "What is it?"

"It's an NDA agreement. Better late than never."

Stunned, Amalia took the documents from him. "What

will you do if I break it? Sue me? I have nothing but pencil skirts and a savings account that's dwindling by the hour."

"I will tie you to a court case in Khaleej for the rest of your lifetime."

"Then I'll tell the—"

"You seem to think we're on an even keel with each other. This meeting was about setting the rules. Just because I answered your questions and laugh at your quips does not mean I will lose sight of our objective. Do not threaten me again, Amalia.

"I have more power. I will always have more power in this relationship. Please me with your performance these next few months and I will see your brother released if he's innocent."

"You're a bully, Sheikh."

"If that's what you need to call me to understand the situation, so be it." If looks could kill, Zayn had a feeling he would be ashes now. "Did you contact your father?"

A different kind of tension filled her body, her mouth flattening into a thin line. "No."

"You do not think you should let him know some version of the truth before he sees it plastered across some social media site? You are, after all, his daughter."

"He won't care."

"I am sure he will—"

"I won't be told what to do in this, Sheikh. I don't care if you throw me in jail for the rest of my life. I'm not answerable to him. And I'm answerable to you only as long as Aslam is in jail.

"And speaking of whom, I have to see him before I leave."

"Not possible. I will not risk you leaking everything I'm trying to hold intact in an emotional moment with your brother. Believe me, Amalia, Aslam is barely suffering where he is. In fact, this might be a good lesson in growing up for your brother."

"That's not for you to decide."

"It will be precisely I who decides if your performance is not up to the mark." He tugged until she fell against him with a throaty gasp. "You should start practicing calling me Zayn. I do demand respect from my future wife. But I do not want the world to think she's terrified of me."

Outrage flashed in her eyes and her mouth curved into a snarl. "I hate you, Zayn. How does that sound?"

Letting her go, Zayn laughed. Now, all he had to remember was that Amalia was still a wild card, the wildest bet he had ever made in his life.

He didn't doubt for a minute that she would leak the entire story to a rapt news reporter in the future if she thought it to her advantage, if this whole issue of her brother's case was not resolved to her satisfaction.

The threat she represented was enough to douse Zayn's interest like a dip in that cold pool. He would have to ensure that she didn't remain a threat to his reputation, or Mirah's happiness, even Khaleej's stability.

"I think I should tell Massi the truth."

"What have you told him so far?"

"I emailed him that certain things were going out of my control. That I would not be able to return in a month."

Every time she mentioned her boss's name, he felt a tight knot in his gut. "And?"

She sighed. "And if I know Massi and I do, he's not going to like it. Neither is he going to believe that I fell in love with you so suddenly. It is better I tell him the truth— that this is nothing but a show."

"Absolutely not." Zayn moved closer to her, the tanned sheen of her smooth skin an invitation. But he resisted the urge to find out if it was as smooth as it looked. "This is between only you and me, Amalia. Not even my closest adviser is going to know that beneath your prim manner is a cunning blackmailer.

"Whatever relationship you had with Massi was finished the moment you considered blackmailing me."

Taking her to bed, much as his body was already weaving fantasies about it, was not an option.

And with the media frenzy surrounding him being what it was, he could not go near a woman until all this was wrapped up to his satisfaction.

Whether he liked it or not, celibacy, for at least a few months, seemed to be the order of the day. *Never succumb to weakness or another's will*, had been beat into him from a young age. He played hard because he needed to let loose, to cope with the pressures of his life, not because he was of weak will.

A few months with a fake, extremely annoying fiancée was a short price to pay to ensure Mirah's happiness.

CHAPTER FIVE

AMALIA TRIED TO restore some calm through her usual breathing exercises on the Al-Ghamdi private jet as she and Zayn winged their way to Paris ten days later, but the ritual that had always helped her maintain composure in the face of her mother's swinging moods and her declining health in the last two years, failed to help her at all.

She was anxious about Aslam, about the coming charade, about her attraction to the man on the opposite side of the craft and even being equipped with all the tools to face the world and the media as the playboy sheikh's adoring fiancée didn't help a bit with that anxiety.

Ten days in which a stylist and a beautician had been sent to bring her up to scratch. She wouldn't have admitted it to Zayn under the promise of death, but Amalia had loved the Parisian stylist and her chic sense of style. Instead of forcing her views on how the sheikh's supposed fiancée should look, the woman had helped Amalia choose dresses and accessories that fit her sense of style. It had been like being on one of those super-trendy makeover shows without the cringe worthy being-on-TV part.

No expense had been spared on her new wardrobe, which included only designer dresses and shoes, handbags and even hats for different occasions. It was neatly stowed away at the back of the luxurious jet. A square-cut diamond in a solitaire setting had been delivered to her suite, with the same aplomb as a non-fiction book she'd requested. Hoping that it would fit all wrong so that she could send it back, she'd been dismayed when it slid on perfectly.

Now its cold weight on her finger felt like a chain around her neck, a constant reminder that she was taking part in a dangerous charade.

Refusing to give in to Zayn's all too possessive and personal order to not cut her hair, Amalia had asked the woman if a shorter hairstyle would serve her better and had received a very stringent, almost offended reply in return.

The stylist had fingered her long locks and told her she had hair like spun gold and it would be blasphemy to the hair gods to cut it off. Instead she had cut it into layers so that the shortest framed Amalia's face. Again, Amalia couldn't ignore the fact that it had been something she had been meaning to do for years and had not gotten to it.

From then on, she had realized it was a waste of energy to protest and had thrown herself into it, at least the whipping-her-into-shape part, with proper gusto. She had been given a mud bath, a facial, a manicure and pedicure, in short, pampered from head to toe like never before.

The servants, obviously under the orders of the imperious Sheikh, packed away her work clothes. It felt as if her armor was being torn away from her. His comment that Amalia always dressed to hide herself hit her hard.

Had she been doing that? she wondered for the hundredth time.

All she'd received when she'd boarded the jet had been a cursory look from Zayn and a condescending nod as if to say he found her acceptable.

She was clearly losing her marbles because she'd been disappointed by that cursory look. Greedy for more, she had hunted down that *Celebrity Spy!* article again and apparently, Sheikh Zayn preferred sophisticated, confident women who knew all the rules of the game. Women who probably didn't run hot and cold at the idea of just one kiss, much less panicked about being his partner, even for a short while.

If Amalia had any doubts about whether he was attracted to her in any way, her meeting with his sister Mirah had put paid to that. Mirah had not just been surprised but shocked when he had introduced Amalia as his fiancée. Granted, some of it had been because of how sudden their engagement was. "You are a career woman. Wow, my brother truly does not realize what has hit him, yes? I have always felt sadness that Zayn would not even consider love as a factor into his marriage. But you...clearly, love is the only reason he chose you," she had said with a beaming smile on her face.

Just then, Amalia found herself chewing on those words. Why was it sad that Mr. Alpha Sheikh did not want love in his marriage? He probably knew any woman would run far and fast at the idea of loving him and had suitably adjusted his expectations.

As though called, pulled toward him by some invisible rope, Amalia found her gaze moving toward him. Thankfully, his dark head was bent to his laptop and she studied him greedily.

The wide breadth of his shoulders against the compact design of the jet's seat, the lean, powerful line of his thighs—Amalia got warm in her silk suit just looking at him.

The sleeves of his light blue dress shirt were rolled up to his elbows, displaying olive-skinned arms with a generous sprinkling of hair. Papers were strewn over the desk in front of him. Long fingers, fingers that had tugged at her hair, fingers that had rasped over her cheeks, tapped away at the keyboard in a somewhat stultifying way. As if he didn't quite know how to type.

The deepening scowl on his face made Amalia smile with a wicked joy. Apparently, Mr. Sheikh was not perfect at everything. She stood up from her seat and took the one opposite him. Even with the spacious seating and her adjusting her legs, her knees bumped against his. "Need a little help, Sheikh?"

He looked up, and for once his focus on her was a bit diluted. Good, she could handle him like this. "One of my PAs fell sick at the last minute and one has to stay behind in Sintar to deal with any contingencies. And the third one is useless. All she does is blush and mutter incoherently every time she lays eyes on me. I would have fired her if I hadn't been assured again and again by the rest of the staff that she's utterly efficient and hardworking in my absence."

He sounded so disgruntled but she couldn't manage a smile. "It must be a curse to be such a perfect specimen of manhood," she said a little acidly.

"You're more nuisance than a help. So return to your seat, say very little and just look perfect for the rest of the flight. Let us call it your job description for the next few months." His gaze turned away dismissively. "That pantsuit, while sufficient, is not good enough for the fundraiser."

Amalia swallowed the growl that wanted to rise from the depths of her soul. The dismissive prig! "I feel sorry for the woman who ends up marrying you, Sheikh."

"Don't. Some women like having a man who will take care of their every need."

A part of her was more than tempted to leave him to his hell, but a part of her, the part that had become extremely bored over the past ten days and the part that was acutely aware that there were six hours and eight more minutes left on the flight, and the stubborn part that wanted to prove something of herself to him said, "That software you're struggling with, we use the same program to manage Massi's schedule."

"It's not just the schedule. I need these reports sorted by urgency and importance and summarized for me. Not everything needs to end up on my desk. There are different departments that most of these requests can be routed to."

"Believe me, Sheikh, I can do all that, too."

"Why are you offering to help?"

"Even though you have been an utter a—" he raised that imperious brow again and she changed her word "—beast to me, you mean?"

"Did you talk this way to your Massi?"

She shrugged, refusing to accept or deny. Damn it, she should have never hinted as if there was more to it. "I'm offering to help because there are a million minutes to pass before we reach Paris and I've been twiddling my thumbs for ten days. Believe me, a makeover that you don't have to pay for is all well and good but I've never been this idle for so long. I'm bored to death and the guards you have on me don't even know how to play cards."

"They're not for your entertainment, Amalia." He let his gaze sweep over her face, something challenging in it. "There are all kinds of state programs here. And you did refuse to sign the NDA. How do I know you're not collecting material for your next blackmail scheme?"

Amalia didn't know why his lack of trust in her should pinch her so. Really, it seemed she was existing in some dream land. Why did she again and again find herself surprised by what a hard man he was? Why was it that she weakened with him when no other man had even come close?

She sat back in her seat, waiting for that emotional reaction to subside before she spoke. "You either trust me over the next few months, Sheikh, or you do not. Like you were so careful to point out, I have no power in this relationship. And everything to lose.

"You can dress me in the fanciest clothes and threaten me with everything from jail to incarceration, but no one is going to believe this charade until you trust me. And you treat me, *no, at least pretend* like you value my place in your life."

"Of course you were feeling neglected. Once we return, I will arrange a vacation for you." Having her out of his hair, under surveillance, Zayn congratulated himself on thinking of it. It was the best way to minimize the damage she could do to the situation with her loud mouth.

That he was hiding from the problem was something Zayn refused to even consider.

"You're not packing me off to Siberia with two guard dogs. The one thing I wanted was to visit with Aslam and you vetoed it." She snorted. "I have worked for five years for a man who controls a million-dollar business. You… you pretty much run the country. I think I can imagine what a working day for you constitutes. I'm not complaining, just informing you."

"You are different from any woman I have ever known, Amalia."

If she had to hear that one more time, Amalia was going to scream. "So you keep reminding me, Sheikh. And the message has been noted, loud and clear. Now can we move on?"

"I will arrange for you to visit Aslam once we return to Sintar. On your word that you will not reveal anything of our agreement to him."

Now it was her turn to be shocked. "Clever move,

Sheikh. Dangle the carrot in front of the poor donkey. You're only using that to keep me in line."

"Now who has trust issues?"

The silence that descended was strained with so many things that Amalia looked away.

"Is it only me and what I provoke in you that has made you so combative, Amalia, or are you like that with all men, including your Massi?"

"He is not my Massi and I…they call me Calm in the Storm back at work. Did you know that?"

"I'd have just called you the storm. So it is me, then."

Such asinine satisfaction drawled in his words that Amalia wanted to do something violent. Which would only confirm his arrogant theory. She was a little afraid to test it, too. "We got off to the wrong start, yes. Which is why I think it is time to call truce," Amalia finished, admitting to herself that she had provoked him from the moment she had set eyes on him.

And to be brutally honest, he had behaved like a gentleman even though he had every reason to doubt her. Except the kiss. She still had no idea what that was about.

She stuck out her hand over the small table between them. "Since I'm not the type to hold a grudge, I'm waving a white flag… *Zayn*."

His name on her lips reverberated through the entire craft, as if some invisible barrier had been smashed, leaving something else in the air around them.

Amalia met his gaze and saw the infinitesimal widening of those dark eyes, before he lowered them to look at her hand. Slowly, he made contact with her right hand.

A curious swooping sensation in her gut, she suddenly wished she hadn't forced the issue. Only now when it was too late, did she realize that the sheikh and she being at each other's throats covered up a lot of things she didn't want to face.

Like her increasing attraction to him.

Suddenly, it felt like it was written all over her face and in the stilted silence between them. Just as she was about to stand up, he leaned forward in his seat, his legs bracketing hers on either side. "I do not know that I prefer my name on your lips, Amalia."

"Exactly what I was thinking. I think I'll stick to Sheikh."

Confined to her seat by his large body, Amalia shivered. Her breath was a languorous fire in her throat, her pulse skittering madly as his finger traced the veins on her wrist.

She'd never been so afraid to look into a man's eyes and see what they held, never been afraid of what was written in her own eyes.

He turned his laptop so that the screen was facing her. The software program she had claimed she was an expert on could have been written in Arabic for all she could make sense of it. "I will go through each of these and dictate notes about who should address it and the steps that need to be taken. Start typing."

She looked up then, shock stealing her words.

He raised those dark brows, the hard mouth twitching at the sides. "Problems already?"

Pulling her watch and bracelets off, Amalia put them in a corner of the desk and straightened in her seat. Tugging the rubber band she'd been playing with through her fingers, she pushed back her hair and gathered it in one hand.

A hard glitter in his eyes, the way he followed her movements, sent a pulse of longing through Amalia. It was hard to be in the company of a compellingly attractive man like the sheikh and not feel a feminine flutter. To not imagine all sorts of romantic illusions even if one tried to be sensible.

Indulging in a moment of weakness didn't mean she would pursue anything, Amalia told herself. Not that the sheikh wanted a personal anything with her. He barely trusted her, did he?

So Amalia clung to what did make sense. She opened a new Notes window and smiled at him. "I'm ready when you are, Sheikh."

CHAPTER SIX

THREE... THERE WERE three small white pearl buttons on Amalia's pink pantsuit and they were driving Zayn to distraction.

Every time she moved in her seat, which she did constantly, the thin blouse she wore under the deeply cut jacket stretched sinuously against her breasts.

It was the same every day, his awareness of her growing by the minute.

He fisted his hands by his sides, fighting the urge to fill his hands with something else. He had seen women wearing skimpily provocative clothes and still somehow look less sensual than the woman working away on his laptop, her brow tied in concentration.

Her long hair pulled into a high ponytail swung as her fingers raced over the keyboard.

The pantsuit was the height of designer chic, taking advantage of the long line of her legs. When she'd come aboard the jet, Zayn had felt a wave of startling awareness again. He'd heard reports from his senior aide and had chosen to avoid her, all the while telling himself that he was just too busy.

Now he knew why he had avoided her.

Ten days had not dimmed her appeal one bit.

From the buttons to the narrow collar to the silk that

didn't quite hug her curves, it was Amalia to a T—prim, buttoned up and yet utterly provocative.

He shouldn't be surprised by anything this woman did and yet Zayn was. He wasn't quite sure what to expect from her. What had she called the house? The perfect marriage of tradition and modernity?

Not even Mirah had seen his struggle reflected in his design. He, who prided himself on knowing himself and his mind, even he had missed it.

Her attire was the perfect blend of sophistication and the demureness that he sensed was an innate part of Amalia. That she'd managed to retain a sense of her own style and self under the obvious duress she felt at being his fiancée, at being thrust into the eye of the media from her average life, spoke to the strength of her personality.

By now, Zayn would have written off any other woman with such decidedly strong views. Yet, Amalia continued to persist in his mind and body.

Utterly covered up as every inch of her skin was, it still hadn't stopped him from losing his focus more than once. Her skin gleamed with the tan she had acquired, no doubt trudging through the city streets of Sintar and harrying unsuspecting males into answering her questions about her twin.

Even now, all he could think of was unbuttoning those buttons slowly while he kissed every inch of the silky-smooth skin he exposed.

He'd always compartmentalized his private life and his public one. Which was why everyone including his father and Farid's family had been so thoroughly shocked at some of the lurid stuff that *Celebrity Spy!* had said about him.

This had to be the same. Amalia was part of his public life, even though his reasons were personal. Ergo, he couldn't indulge in fantasies about her.

"Okay, how does this sound?" she interrupted him, her brow thoughtful. And then rattled off the press release she had volunteered to put together about a donation he was making to the Sintar General Hospital.

"It's perfect," he said, a little jolted again at the quiet efficiency with which she finished her tasks. Apparently, the woman was just as good at her job as she had claimed. Could he believe her word that he could trust her? "We'll break for lunch and start in a half hour again."

"No, I want to finish this summary for why you're denying the proposal for the Art and Education Center in downtown Sintar."

With a shrug, Zayn leaned back in his seat. He checked his watch and realized that they had been at it for three hours without a break.

Once he had realized how supremely capable she was, there had been no point in not using her abilities.

And of course, Amalia being Amalia didn't work in silence or peace. She offered opinions, sometimes in drastic opposite to his, and to their mutual shock, thoroughly agreeing with him on some foreign policy matter.

Piles of what he'd considered boring, menial tasks had been completed in a most engaging way, thanks to her efficiency and her interesting opinions.

True to her word, she hadn't even blinked at the grueling pace he had set. For a woman who wasn't aware of the intricacies of palace policy, she'd learned the administration's priorities and his personal policies on some of the administrative matters superfast. But of course, he had forgotten that she was very learned about Khaleej and its history and politics.

He wasn't fooled by her rejection of everything that was her father's heritage. Her anger only hid some deeprooted pain but Zayn had no need to know or understand what it stemmed from. Her issues with her father were of no interest to him except for how they affected the outcome he wanted.

Amazing as it was that it had come from her, she was right. They needed to call a truce, if he wanted to pull this off. But the truce did not have to extend to exchanging their every dream and fear. She had surprised him that day in his wing but he would not veer off course again.

Zayn had never been allowed a confidant before and he was too rigid in his ways to want one now.

He ordered lunch and drinks for both of them just as Amalia finished and looked up. The little knot in her brow and the way she met his gaze head-on, he knew she was going to disagree with him again.

He had never met a more opinionated woman in his life. Raising a hand, he preempted her. The tight purse of her mouth made him smile. "I know you're about to launch into one of your lengthy opinions about what an old, dying beast Sintar and its administrative policy is, but I'm famished."

"Your country is a contradiction, Sheikh. Just like you are."

Did the woman not know her limits? Or was this her agenda, to infuriate and annoy him so much that he released her brother? "My country, Amalia?"

She raised a brow casually while her up-tilted chin betrayed her defiance. Two could play at the perception game, he decided with a smile.

"This will only take a minute, and the food is not here yet. And really, Sheikh, I didn't realize that your ego needed so much validation that you only surround yourself with yes-men."

He sighed. For all she looked like an angelic wraith, the woman was like a pit bull when she got her teeth into something. "Go ahead. You have three minutes before you lose my attention."

"That's not enough!"

"That's how long people usually have to convince me."

"You're a—"

"Two minutes and counting."

She looked down at the screen and back at him, determination written all over her face. "I don't think you should refuse to fund the Arts and Education Foundation in Sintar. Khaleej needs the kind of human development this foundation promises."

The depth of her passion reminded Zayn of himself when he had been younger and idealistic. For all she seemed self-sufficient, there was a charming naïveté to her. "Those funds will be more useful channeled toward health care. Education Reform will get its time."

"But you just signed off on what equates—" she scrunched her brow and Zayn's mouth twitched "—to ten million dollars for just the next three years toward reforms in health care."

"I just proposed it. The cabinet will still have to approve it. And the reason you're interested in that foundation is because it promises the kind of academic freedom for both sexes in all fields that is seen in the West. As progressive as my father and I have been, things move slowly here. I will alienate a bunch of cabinet members if I give the green signal on that."

"I say this threefold mission of education, scientific research and community development is just as necessary for Sintar. I've seen the development in infrastructure and health care in the two months I've been here. And I know that it is all attributable to you, Zayn, but Khaleej is going to be left behind in the global world if it does not also embrace a more global approach toward arts and education.

This wealth that Khaleej enjoys because of its oil and gas reserves is not going to last long.

"You will need an educated, qualified workforce that includes both sexes if Khaleej wants to continue its current healthy financial growth, and this center seems to be the right step in that direction."

"You are very passionate about this. Why?"

"Does there have to be a reason for pure common sense?"

"The more something is important to you, the more flippant you get. If that is your answer—"

"There is no other reason than that women should be allowed to pursue academic interests just as men do."

"Is that what your mother and father split about?" The question fell from his mouth despite his intention to stay out of her personal matters.

A bitterness he didn't like seeing at all entered her beautiful eyes. "For as long as I can remember of their marriage even before they divorced, they fought about everything. Prestige and perception was a big deal to my father and his family, and he forbade her from going back to her former profession. Her definition in life was to be a wife and mother. As long as her ambition or her dream did not interfere with those duties, she was allowed to have them."

Her placid eyes blazed when she said *forbade*. Within minutes, she transformed from an efficient PA to a tigress.

"How old were you when they divorced?"

"Thirteen."

"You were a mere child, Amalia. Things always look black-and-white. How can you be so sure why their marriage fell apart?"

"Because I was the one who lived with the fallout. For years, I listened to her while she…she grieved the loss of him."

"What was her profession?"

"She was a model at the height of her career when she met him."

"Then he was right to forbid her."

"Of all the—"

"This is not our fight, Amalia. But I'm being realistic. Professor Hadid is a venerated historian, a man with a powerful public image. Your mother would have known the sacrifices she'd have to make when she married him. I cannot see how she thought she could continue with such a controversial career and still be his wife."

"I don't think she cared so much about the modeling as much as being boxed in the little space he had for her in his life, the little he allowed her to do. That they were both strong personalities and came from different cultures, I'm sure, didn't help. It's a wonder that they fell in love at all."

"Lots of couples mistake good old lust with love. It is possible—"

Defiance radiated off her. And it was vulnerability, pain, that she hid beneath that defiance. "She never stopped loving him. Not until her last breath last year. He never once…" She closed her eyes, fighting for control over herself. "She made herself weak by loving him while he remarried and just made himself a new family."

Something in her tone broke through Zayn's hands-off policy and he clutched her hand on the desk.

The jolt from the contact was instant. Never had he felt a connection like this before. The more he tried to ignore it, the sharper his awareness of her became. Her hand was soft and slender in his big one and yet, there was strength in her grip.

Eyes wide pools in her face locked with his, brimming with emotion. The rawness of it went through Zayn like lightning shifted the entire picture of the sky. Her hand gentled in his, a little trusting, a little searching, and he felt some core of ice inside him, a place that he hadn't even known existed, thaw a little.

This new emotion that surged through him, urging him to take her in his arms...was this tenderness for her?

"Was her passing hard for you?"

She shrugged and pulled her hand from his. When she looked at him again, there was none of that vulnerability in her eyes. Curiously, Zayn felt both relief and a strange sense of loss. As if he had been granted a glimpse of something intense, something real, something he had never known before but it was taken away from him before he could fully comprehend it.

He wasn't sure he wanted to see that vulnerability in her eyes again. For it made him forget that she was not to be trusted.

"She gave up on life a long time ago." Guilt pinched her features. "Is it horrible of me to say I felt a sense of relief when the end came?"

Zayn could not answer her. Why had her father not shared this responsibility with her? If not for his wife, he still had some duty owed to his daughter. Even his parents, who were coldly practical with their own children and barely had any time or interest in parenting him or Mirah, still made sure they were taken care of by others.

He had been taught early on in life that he wasn't supposed to have any emotional vulnerability. And he completely agreed with that policy for someone in his position. Whereas Amalia, he was realizing, had seen only that in her parent.

"Just because he remarried does not mean he did not love her." He gritted his teeth hearing how sentimental he sounded.

Damn it, he had no taste for playing a hero, *her hero*,

and he was sure as the bright desert sun neither did Amalia want one.

"Whether he truly loved her at all, now that…I doubt." Challenge glimmered in her eyes. "Powerful men, men who are used to having the world at their feet, I fear, will say and do anything to have a woman they fancy. Did you know my father is a great lover of objects of beauty? I remember our home used to be littered with them, people from all over the country coming to see him. I have no doubt he thought her another collectible he should own. When she refused to sit on the shelf he provided for her, he discarded her."

And me. The unsaid words hung in the air, full of a pain she would never admit to. The more he learned of her, the more Zayn was sure that Amalia was one of those complex women he had no use for.

Still, the depth of her bitterness stunned him. "That is a twisted view to have of one's father."

"It's a realistic view of my father and what love can do when it is not returned in the same way. Don't tell me that you're a closet romantic, Sheikh. That you're privately agonizing over having to choose a docile, traditional bride." A brittle smile came to her lips, a determined glint in her eyes.

Her little remark bounced off his hide. "I heartily agree with you that the whole concept of love only complicates marriage. My parents' marriage is a success only because they had no expectations of each other. And so no complaints, either."

"What does that mean?"

"They married because it was an advantageous match for both of them. My father would get a bride from an aristocratic family and she her own sphere of powerful people to command. An heir for the country was the one common goal and once they had me, they pursued their own lives. My father had his mistress and his politics, and my mother, her own pursuits. Everything else, even Mirah, was a byproduct of the main goal of the marriage."

The look in her eyes made Zayn laugh. It was refreshing and a little addictive to see a woman not cater to his personality or his status. But he was sure it would soon lose its charm. Sooner or later, Amalia would lose her appeal to him. He was too used to docile, pleasing women who didn't question their role in his life. After all, no one woman had ever swayed his control, ever. "Why do you look so…combative even when I agree with you?"

"Because that's not what I said at all. That does not sound like marriage at all. That sounds like…a clinical agreement in a science-fiction novel. This is what you're modeling your marriage on, too, isn't it?"

"By all measures, their union continues to be a success, so why not?"

"If you don't even want your wife's companionship, why marry?"

"To produce legitimate heirs."

"And then you set the wife aside?" She didn't even wait for his nod. "Did your mother not mind it? I can't believe that any woman would willingly walk into a marriage like that."

He shrugged. "The number of women Ms. Young found for me says otherwise. As to Mother, if she didn't know it at the beginning, I'm sure she learned it soon."

"I could never marry a man like that."

"My wife will want for nothing. She will never have to work a day in her life, will be independently wealthy beyond imagination and will lead a life of globe-trotting, couture-shopping and feasting on mussels and duck confit of the highest order. And to top it all, she will have me in her bed, for as long as she wants me, to fulfill every little heated fantasy she might have ever had." Zayn had no idea why he was goading her like that, or why he wanted to hear her admit that she wanted him. Was it only a stroke to his ego as she had claimed?

Or was it all the confidences they had exchanged, this talk about marriage and love that stirred something inside him? That gave him a vague sense of disquiet in his gut?

All he knew was that he wanted to muss up Amalia's self-sufficiency, to push past the prickles and see what she was made of beneath it all.

He could see Amalia in that role, especially in that last scene. Amalia, whose heated fantasies he was making true. Amalia, who stared at him with naked longing, her long, silky limbs splayed invitingly over his bed, Amalia submitting that fiery temper and that steel core to him.

"Tell me you're not a little tempted." The hoarse need in his voice shocked him, the languorous heat flaring through him coming up against the self-control he prided himself on.

She tipped her chin, her gaze sweeping over him in a thorough appraisal that Zayn found incredibly arousing. As if she was weighing all the benefits of going to bed with him against everything else, as if she was imagining the same incredibly erotic scene… Was she so thoroughly naive that she didn't know the signals she was sending?

And yet, even as her topaz-colored eyes flared into wide pools, her sensuous lower lip trembled, she would even deny admitting it.

How thoroughly aggravating could this woman be! And yet, Zayn's awareness of her, his desire for her, only grew sharper.

He had months of this pretense, months of sparring with this woman before he would be able to remove her from his life. Before he could go back to the path that had been decided for him even before he'd been born.

Her openly hungry gaze said she was more than tempted, by him at least if not by his wealth, while her lush mouth said, "No. Not in the least bit. I have no romantic illusions, but I want a marriage between equals. I want affection, respect, a man who will deem my ambitions equally important as his own."

"That will never work in reality. Even if my duty to Khaleej didn't come before my personal desires, I would always be the aggressor in my relationship with a woman."

He saw the tremor that went through her slender shoulders, the shift to sensible reality as her gaze cleared. "Fortunately, not every man on the planet is so rampantly, aggressively masculine that he demands complete submission in every aspect of life, including..."

"Including?"

She looked at him and then away, but he caught her glance. Abashed.

The sound of his laughter reverberated in the confines of the jet. Feral satisfaction coated every breath he released as color poured into her cheeks. Her mouth pursed, her eyes flashing topaz fire at him, her lithe body radiating barely suppressed outrage, she made a delicious picture.

Zayn had never been so satisfied that his *aggressive masculinity* apparently could drive a woman nuts. Nor had the exposé been the source of anything but a headache. Until now. "So how many times did you read the part about my...voracious appetites?"

He wondered if smoke would come out of her ears if he teased her any more. "It's not a compliment, Sheikh," she offered in a dull voice. "It's more...a statement of fact."

"What will you do if you never find this ideal man?"

She shrugged, but by the little frown on her head, Zayn

knew she had never really thought about any of this. He wondered if her mother's poison had forever turned her off men, or if it was justification to never commit herself to one man. That meant she was either untouched or was one of those modern women who could have sex for the pleasure it afforded. Like he did.

Utterly hypocritical of him, but even in this indulgent speculation, Zayn found he preferred the first option far better than the second when it came to Amalia. He, who had always welcomed sophisticated and sexually mature women into his bed, women who knew what they would get from him.

What was beyond disturbing, however, was that his... *interest* in her didn't wane either way. The growing realization that Amalia might be innocent should have been a deterrent. It had been before, for he was not a man from whom women could expect flowers, or gentle kisses or wooing. Jewelry, designer clothes, the right word in a highly connected ear, and mind-blowing sex—that was more his forte. For the first time since he'd come into his own, Zayn had a sense of inadequacy, for Amalia wanted nothing he could give.

"I'm far too busy with my career right now anyway. And if I can't meet a man like that, I guess I'll stay single." Did she know how dejected she sounded at the end there? That her eyes ate him away even as she challenged him?

He leaned in, trapping her in her seat. She was forced to spread her legs to accommodate his frame, and the warmth of her body was a teasing rasp against his own. "You work all kinds of hours, you want this impossibly ideal man to marry. What will you do in the meantime?"

Her tongue snaked out and licked at that lush lower lip, while her gaze locked with his. "In the..." a little throaty rasp, "in the meantime? What does that mean?"

"What about passion, Amalia? What do you do when you get lonely at night, or when your body demands a certain kind of satisfaction that only a man can give?"

He leaned in a little more until his breath feathered over the rim of her ear. A little tremor shook her shoulders, her fingers tight over the armrest. Something she had dabbed on her pulse point in her neck floated up at the warmth of her skin, the scent incredibly arousing. God, did she smell like that all over? "Are you telling me you've never felt even a little stirring of sexual hunger? Or do you take lovers just for that purpose and discard them when you're done?"

"Passion is overrated," she whispered, and her breath caressed his cheek. In utter contrast to her words, her fingers rose to his cheeks, traced the line of his jaw. "All my life—" tips painted the palest pink now moved to the edge of his mouth and started tracing the curve of his lower lip "—I've seen the toxic effect it could have, not on one or two, but four lives."

Zayn felt like a predator caged and forced to sheath his claws while his favorite prey sniffed out around him. He wanted her hands on his hot skin, his tight muscles, those questing fingers on the part of him that was thickening in reaction to her touch. "But what about passion shared between two people who have no expectations of each other except mutual pleasure?" The question fell from his mouth before he realized he was asking it.

Naked longing swept across her face as her gaze rested on his mouth. "I've never…been tempted to throw caution to the wind."

Until now.

She didn't say the words but her rumbling breath, her trembling mouth, they spoke for her. Her chest fell and rose fast, her mouth moving closer and closer to his. Another breath and he knew he would plumb the taste of her lush mouth.

He tipped her chin up until she was looking into his eyes. Desire had darkened them; her nostrils flared. "If I kiss you now, I will not stop, Amalia. Come to me when you're ready. Come to me when you can admit that you want me."

Before he was tempted to lick the pulse that was hammering madly at her neck, Zayn got up from his seat.

His blood hummed with the thrill of the chase, his muscles tight against the heat flooding his body. He had never played at seduction this way; it had never been a chase like this where he didn't really know how it would end.

He didn't know what he wanted to do with Amalia, only that he wanted to tame that fiery spirit of hers, just a little. To possess a part of her. Maybe like his Bedouin ancestors had done with wild horses.

After all, he raised horses and he knew all too well what an edgy, risky venture it was to conquer the spirit of a high-strung filly without breaking its spirit. That it wasn't about submission but only establishing his dominance over the wild horses. Until they became one.

It was about possessing something wild for a few minutes in one's lifetime; it was about living. He was sure Amalia would club him if she knew that he had compared her to a beast. Amalia, with her stubborn notions and impossible ideals, needed to be shown how to live a little.

He had months yet with her, a devilish voice whispered in his mind but he squashed it for now. As he reached the entrance to the rear cabin, he turned.

She was still sitting in the seat, quite as he had left her, her chest still rising and falling. "Amalia?" he prompted

"Hmm?" She looked up with a start and then blushed profusely. He let the amusement that filled him curve his lips, knowing it would aggravate her even more. Soft and vulnerable and a little too dazed to keep up her prickly defenses, he liked her like this. A lot. And from there, it was only a quick slide for his mind to imagine how she would be sated and pliable in his arms. Under his aching body. In his bed with her golden hair spread over his pillow.

"Do not forget to finish the rest of the correspondence, yes? You look a little lost there."

He didn't wait to see her expression. But he could feel her glare on his back, could imagine the steely set of her shoulders return. Zayn whistled a tune he didn't even know he'd remembered, feeling lighter than he had felt in a long time.

CHAPTER SEVEN

AMALIA HAD SPENT most of the week meeting more people than she'd ever want to meet in her entire life. The luxury hotel Zayn and she were staying at, while sharing the same suite, had views of the Seine and the Eiffel Tower on either side.

In the week since they had arrived here, they had been to a movie premiere and then reception with A-list stars, taken a quick flight to Dublin at predawn so that he could visit a stud farm on the outskirts of the city to buy a filly called Desert Night because apparently, her fiancé was not only a brilliant architect but also an expert on horse breeding and owned a world-class stud farm in Sintar, gone to a trade summit with some European leaders, and the culmination of the week was to be a charity fund-raiser at the Four Seasons in Paris again.

Of course, there was media coverage of their every movement. And the wave of news began from the fact that Amalia had been the only woman to have ever been the sheikh's partner for more than two days in a row. At the movie reception she had been called the sheikh's new arm candy. After returning from the stud farm, she'd been called his new mistress. At the trade summit, they had speculated that maybe she was the sheikh's new PA/lover.

Because of course what hardworking prince of the coun-

try didn't want to save money with a convenient woman doing double duty as both PA and lover... She'd made the tart remark thoroughly frustrated and overwhelmed by the press's interest in him and them.

"Should I be paying you double, then?" he'd said with a devilish twitch to that hard mouth that had made Amalia's knees wobble. When he smiled like that with that amused gleam in his eyes, the panorama of his entire face changed. And Amalia's resistance to him slipped a little.

Somehow she'd had enough working cells in her brain to throw a pillow at him across the room and retort, *"You don't pay me even for one role, Sheikh."*

His languid gaze had crept over her modest dressing gown that didn't cover her wobbly knees, her vanity's weakest point, and her horrible bed head until her pulse leaped into her throat. *"You'll let me know if you're interested in joining my staff or my bed, won't you, Azeezi?"*

Her heart thudding violently against her rib cage, Amalia had thrown the next thing she could find, her hairbrush, across the room. Laughing, he'd ducked in a graceful movement and said, *"You're exactly like Desert Night, Amalia. Prickly and wild-tempered."*

She had stood there a full five minutes after he'd left, the suite's silence amplifying what had to be the most absurd question she'd ever asked herself.

Had he been only joking? Did he really want her? Damn it, why wasn't she sophisticated enough to just ask?

But even the thought of showing her slowly fluttering interest in him sent Amalia into an ice-cold sweat. What if he rejected her and laughed at her? What if he was disappointed with her, the sexual sophisticate that he was?

The worst—what if he...had sex with her, was through with her the next morning and then expected her to continue their pretense like nothing intimate had happened between them?

Fortunately, she had very little time to think these roundabout, frustrating thoughts. The shock that she'd even considered it remained with her for the rest of the day.

Every movement of his and, therefore, hers, was so thoroughly followed that Amalia couldn't breathe in the whirlwind the first three days. Arrogantly ignoring her protests, Zayn had arranged for a PR and social media expert to coach her every day on how to manage her responses, on dealing with suddenly being the media's darling because apparently, only after three different appearances on Zayn's arm, her sense of style had been labeled stellar and unique, and on to how present even the best profile to the press.

Thanks to the prep and her own years of experience in dealing with a super-busy job and her mother's deteriorating health, Amalia hadn't blinked at the endless lessons in etiquette and protocol and the crash course in Khaleej's politics.

"For a woman who snuck into my office only two weeks ago, you're very good at handling this," Zayn had said, a grudging admiration in his eyes when Amalia had smoothly cut off a reporter for asking her about her fiancé's tastes for multiple bed partners.

The question had unraveled a disquiet in her gut, only she'd gotten better at hiding it. At examining it in the relative privacy of her bedroom at night, an all too familiar restlessness in her limbs.

The very idea of Zayn's colorful sexual life, the images supplied by her overactive mind, began to leave a bitter distaste in her mouth, a dark emotion whirling in her gut.

The media coverage didn't make Zayn even blink. He wouldn't have cared about the lurid exposé, either, if it hadn't affected Mirah's wedding. And if not for the pressure of the article, he would've had her thrown out of the palace and she would have missed this glimpse into his world, the different facets of the man beneath the sheikh.

Something, Amalia realized, was beginning to enthrall her more and more.

And when he wasn't attending dinners and lunches, the man worked like a demon. Of course, Amalia had known this and matched his punishing pace without a complaint.

She'd never lacked in confidence in her ability to do her job, but the respect she saw growing in such a brilliant man's eyes made Amalia feel as if she could conquer the world.

Every single night, he'd asked Amalia if she was up to working with him for a few hours. Always work with him, he'd say. He'd even started asking for her unbiased, bluntly honest opinion, as he'd taken to calling it on most matters. Those ended up being Amalia's favorite times she spent with him. For even though he was still the sheikh and she his unofficial PA, they quickly began to build a rapport with each other.

When he'd shared the blueprints for the trade and commerce center in Sintar, she'd been dazzled by the scope of it. When she'd asked him who was designing it, his expression had shuttered before he had answered that it was a firm out of London.

But it was the time when they weren't working and they weren't in the public that became the hardest. Even though those moments were few and far between.

No public declaration had been made, too tacky for the sheikh's personal team to cater to the media, she'd been told, and yet the flash of diamond on her finger after a week spent in Paris, the most romantic city in the world, and the fact that she appeared with the sheikh at every event, had done the deed.

Amalia Christensen was now the fiancée of Sheikh Zayn Al-Ghamdi. The evening when the story had hit the press, Amalia couldn't focus.

With a sigh, Zayn had looked up from his laptop after she'd asked him to repeat something a second time. Scolded herself for being so weak, after all these years. "You're restless tonight."

She shrugged, trying to make light of it. "I'm—"

Perceptive brown eyes stayed on her as Amalia tried to erect her defenses. "You expected your father to call."

"No," she retorted loudly, betraying herself anyway.

"You're determined to hate him for the rest of your life but there could be a hundred reasons he didn't contact you now. And he is a phone call away for you."

His sympathy was unbearable in the face of her foolish, childish hope that her father, at least now that she was engaged to the sheikh, would call and ask about her. The long breath she took forced the lump back down her throat. She lifted her eyes to him and her resolve almost broke at the tenderness in Zayn's. "The past week has been a crazy whirl, Zayn. Can you handle your workload without me tonight?" she forced herself to say.

If he'd forced her to confront her feelings, Amalia was sure she'd have thrown herself at him and sobbed. And the last thing she needed was to weaken, especially in front of a coldly calculating man like him. Fortunately, his answer had been a coolly delivered, "Of course."

And just as she reached the door, he said, "You called me Zayn." She heard his light footsteps on the carpet, felt the heat from his body stroke her back like an intimate caress. "But I have to admit, Amalia, never has my title sounded so good as when it falls from your impertinent mouth."

Amalia didn't turn around, an unexpected bashfulness rooting her to the floor. It seemed that the last and somehow stalwart barrier had been finally razed. He didn't know it but she knew what it signified. She'd seen the man beneath the sheikh and as much as he tried to remove the real him from the man he needed to be, she had seen him. And worse, she was beginning to like the hell out of him.

That was about the only personal exchange they'd had in the whole week.

But as the first week merged into the second and Amalia was so thoroughly integrated into every aspect of his life, a different kind of strain began to descend on her. Like a thread of silk that was stretched too tight and too far.

What the endless number of teams and strategists and PR experts hadn't taught Amalia was how to bear the little touches and intimate glances from the sheikh himself, how not to dissolve into a puddle at all the attention he showed her.

When his rock-hard thigh collided against hers, when his arm draped around her waist, becoming the center of attention for every cell in her, when he ran his shockingly abrasive fingers against her upper arm, almost without his knowledge it seemed, when she had replied to someone's question about Sintar…it was a continual onslaught on her senses.

The boundaries she'd been so sure would come to her aid were already blurring under that dark, perceptive gaze. And yet, he seemed to be utterly unperturbed by the deluge of sensations that seemed to be drowning her.

After hours of perfectly synchronizing their acts, of playing the roles of affianced lovers a bit too well, they returned to their suite, and their masks fell away.

The easy camaraderie they shared through the day disappeared instantly.

Tension corkscrewed in the air around them, and more than once, Amalia had wondered desperately if it was only she who felt it. He ignored her so thoroughly in those moments that in contrast, thoughts of him and them began to consume Amalia.

She didn't fit into his life, in any way, she kept reminding herself, but it didn't stop her from imagining them as a couple.

His comments about her appearance were always polite, impersonal, just adequate. Which perversely made her pay even more attention to her outfit and her makeup and her hair. Only to be disappointed again and again at his changing behavior toward her in the last week.

While the little bits and pieces of information she hoarded about him made her own attraction to him more and more consuming.

That he was a ruthless boss but a fair one, too.

That beneath the cloak of power he wore for Khaleej, he was at heart still a dreamer.

"Why do you think I'm in such a hurry to beget sons?" he'd said, when she'd called on his fixation with an heir. *"The moment they're ready, I will pass on the mantle of Khaleej to their capable hands and then I'm going to start my career and live my dream."*

Amalia hadn't had the heart to tell him that she couldn't imagine Zayn ever chucking that duty away, that he'd probably serve Khaleej in one way or the other until his last breath. But then she'd caught a glimpse of a faraway look in his eyes, the hard curve to his mouth as he watched the young apprentice architect describe some building design and she'd realized that he knew.

That the duty-bound, coldly powerful sheikh always, always came first and far behind was Zayn the man himself.

That if, a big *if*, he had felt any attraction to her that first day they had met, he'd have effectively killed it by now because Amalia Christensen didn't fit in to the life of Sheikh Zayn Al-Ghamdi.

It had been a painfully vulnerable moment to witness—she was sure Zayn didn't even realize how well she understood him now—a moment that defined her relationship with him for Amalia, the moment that had brought home pretty hard that at some point, Amalia had started believing in the powerful charade, that she'd passed from attraction to admiration to feeling something much more powerful and terrifying for Sheikh Zayn Al-Ghamdi, the man who found her unsuitable for everything other than posing as his fake fiancée during the day and as his efficient PA at night.

The last night of their two-week itinerary, they were attending a charity fund-raiser gala. The charity named Hope supported young professionals who came from underprivileged backgrounds. Amalia had found it really interesting that four of its most important and generous patrons were the Dirty Four exposed in the *Celebrity Spy!* Article, including Zayn.

When she'd taunted him about how he would know anything about being underprivileged, he'd given her a scathing glance.

Yes, her remark had been irreverent but Amalia's curiosity had been genuine. How could a man who had everything—power, good looks, intelligence—understand someone else? How could a mere woman hope to amount to something to a man like that?

Which was what she'd been doing. And yet, he had proved Amalia wrong.

From his discussion with the patroness to his highly detailed and involved questions about the candidate they'd chosen to receive the scholarship this year, she'd realized this wasn't an impersonal event where he showed his face and disappeared.

Only when Amalia and Zayn had been introduced to a freshly graduated architect before the evening began had she realized the importance of the event and the charity itself to Zayn. This charity was Zayn's project, not the sheikh's.

When she'd asked the thrilled protégé what he was most excited about, his answer had been the project he'd been assigned to in Sintar. Amalia had seen the bittersweet smile in Zayn's face, and for the first time, felt shame at how prejudiced she'd been. Zayn could've become bitter over what he was denied but he'd found a different way to find satisfaction.

Why hadn't her mother done the same? For so many years after they had left Khaleej, Amalia had heard from her mother about all the things her father had forbidden her to do. And yet, she had only wasted her life, filled with that bitterness.

She could have pursued all the things she complained her father hadn't let her do, she could have loved and cherished Amalia, she could have asked Aslam to visit them... instead, she had wallowed in that grief, given up interest on life.

How much of that bitterness had she passed on to Amalia herself?

She'd made so many assumptions about Zayn and he had proved her wrong every time. How many things in life had she denied herself because she had borne witness to her mother's pain and her failures?

That evening she dressed in an ice-blue fitted shift dress

that played hide-and-seek with her knees. The perfect cut made the most of the dip of her waist and the flare of her hip and her legs. It was both trendy and elegant, and Amalia never tired of that style.

Purple pumps had added a flash of color to her outfit. Her thick, wavy hair, had taken two hours to blow dry, straighten and then beat into submission into a chic chignon at the back of her head.

Unlike the last couple of weeks, she found pleasure in dressing up for the evening. Anticipation and excitement made her movements jumpy as she used the naked palettes and a black eyeliner, as the makeup artist had shown her to do, to achieve the kind of glamour she'd only seen on magazine covers before.

And when she had joined Zayn outside the banquet hall where the fund-raiser was being hosted, all of her breath had piled into her throat.

The black tux hugging his wide shoulders and tapering off, he looked like he belonged on the cover of *GQ*. Power and charm radiated from him. A frisson of knee-melting awareness snaked down her spine as he pushed off from the wall.

She was aware of a quiet hush descending around the guests that were already there. Her muscles shook all over, anticipation a bubble in her chest. Even though his gaze swept over her in a leisurely appraisal, all he said was, "You keep getting better and better at this."

Swallowing her disappointment, Amalia stared back at him. It was a wonder she could speak at all. "At what?"

"At this touch-me-not ice-princess image you project. At making me believe that this is the real you." There was a thread of something in his tone that Amalia couldn't quite pin down. At his signal, his junior aide appeared, a box in his hand.

With that arrogance that seemed to be embedded in his very blood, Zayn waited while the man opened the velvet case and extended it toward him, all the while his brown eyes cataloged every small detail about her.

Heat she couldn't fight flooded Amalia at this pointed, masculine appraisal. Her skin felt too tight, her nipples peaking to attention, and a low thrum began to beat in her lower belly. He was doing this on purpose, she realized with a horrified gasp; still, she couldn't stop her reaction.

She would be damned if he let her use her attraction to him as some kind of weapon. Chin tilted, Amalia glared back at him. "If you tell me what I have done to—"

With a flick of his fingers, Zayn dismissed the aide. In the next blink, he had his powerful arms around her and she was drenched in the musky warmth of the man.

Every inch of her skin sang as his hard chest grazed her breasts, his thighs tangled with hers. Tension was so thick around them that she shivered when his fingers rasped against her nape.

The cold slide of something against her neck brought her head down. Diamonds, enough that she couldn't even count, nestled around a delicate platinum wire settled against her heated skin. She fingered the dazzling, multifaceted stones, unable to quell the pleasure that rose through her. The gift didn't matter so much as that he'd put it on. It seemed a romantic gesture although she was the last person who'd know anything about such gestures. "Thank you. I… I'll make sure to…"

His fingers crawled up the sensitive skin of her nape and into her hair, while the other hand remained on her hip. The intimacy of his touch sent her pulse soaring. "It's yours to keep," he whispered at her ear. "I saw it and thought of you."

A sigh escaped her mouth and brought his gaze level

with hers. "You're trembling. Until this evening, I would have bet my kingdom it was me."

His cold tone sliced through the daze her senses seemed to be swimming in. Suddenly, his gift, the possessive way he'd put it on her, everything took on a different meaning. "What are you talking about?"

"Your… Massi is here."

"Here?"

"Mysteriously, yes." The tip of his finger traced the line of her jaw. "Tonight, at the exclusive fund-raiser whose guest list was decided months ago."

Massi was here? In Paris?

A smile came to Amalia's mouth, the thought of a friendly, familiar face filling her with pleasure. A smile that dominated the shock she felt. As far as she knew, Massi was not connected to the Hope charity in any way.

He was here because of her.

Which was exactly what the man in front of her was thinking. Except he'd gone two steps further and come to another conclusion, too.

He didn't come out and say it, but Amalia saw the suspicion in the granite set of his jaw, in the hard contour of his mouth. In the way his beautiful eyes glittered without any real warmth.

The whole necklace and his putting it on her, it had all been a show. The embrace and the intimacy had been his way of staking claim in front of a man he didn't even know. Hurt pinged inside Amalia's chest.

It was her own fault for giving vague answers every time he'd asked about Massi. Now she wanted him to demand answers, to demand his right in her life…

But she would forever be waiting.

Zayn thought of her as the woman who'd blackmailed him. As the woman who wasn't fit to be anything in his life. These two weeks, their exchanges, nothing had significance to the sheikh. For him, it was only a means to achieve his sister's happiness.

The cold kiss of the diamonds on her skin made nausea whirl up through her throat. "If you have something to say, Zayn, say it."

The jut of his stubborn jaw made Amalia want to growl. "No? Then please, let me go so that I can finish this damn pretense and we both can go back to our lives."

Uniformed waiters circulated through the hall, supplying unlimited glasses of champagne. Amalia had sipped a few times from her flute and then passed it back. Even though she'd been sorely tempted to get drunk for the first time in her life and make a spectacle of herself.

That would show the arrogant sheikh how unsuitable she could be.

But too many fates hung in the balance and she decided her little rebellion wouldn't be worth it.

An echo of the frisson that had shot through her when he had seen her went through her again as she looked around the banquet hall and found his dark head.

As if she'd telegraphed it, he looked straight at her and raised his champagne flute. Amalia forced a smile to her lips, a sort of sinking sensation in her stomach. Their little confrontation wasn't over. It hadn't even started, she realized.

He'd only postponed it to the privacy of the night. Because, of course, the sheikh couldn't show even a smidgen of emotion, a weakness in front of the public. Even his anger over her supposed betrayal was under his supreme control, whereas she hadn't been able to hide anything.

What would happen when they went back to the suite they shared?

CHAPTER EIGHT

"I WOULD APPRECIATE it very much if you unhand my fian-cée." Zayn had no idea how he managed to make the warn-ing sound dire when his heart was pounding in his throat. He'd spent a hellish two hours searching for Amalia on the streets of Paris, along with his security team while she…

The fist in his gut would not unclench.

He hadn't known fear like this in…*ever.* The thought of Amalia hurt or worse had consumed him.

He had sworn to fire his entire security team once she had been found. He had called himself a hundred names for not making her aware of what a target she could be to so many different factions now that she belonged to him.

And here she was…in the arms of her lover.

"Stop fondling her at the same time, before some cam-era crew gets a picture of it and plasters it all over social media tomorrow."

"Zayn, I wanted to…"

Her topaz gaze met his in defiance and slowly, softened. Even her temporary yielding did not calm him. Slowly, she moved in the man's embrace, trying to extricate her-self from him. "Massi wanted to catch up and I thought we would have more privacy away from—"

"You will explain later, *habibti*, in the privacy of our suite." A shadow of fear he still could not subdue made his tone harsh. "I have no intention to provide your boss or some other sneaky reporter with a lovers' spat.

"You are a sheikh's fiancée, Amalia. Sneaking out with other men is exactly the kind of fodder that the media looks for."

Her chin tilted up. "Even if it's to catch up with an old—"

"Friend, or ex-lover or your boss…it doesn't matter. After the last two weeks, I thought you understood that. Come, let's return to the suite."

The man turned and looked at Zayn, the cocky tilt of his head deepening the anger in Zayn's stomach. "I'm not done ensuring that Amalia is not with you under some sort of coercion," the Italian replied, his English only slightly accented.

Amalia cringed, but the man's arm did not budge from her waist. "I have already told you the whole story. I know you mean well but Zayn is right."

A tender smile curved the man's mouth, the easy camaraderie between them too obvious to miss. "You have no one else to look after you and…"

Jealousy prowled like a monster in his blood, and it took all of Zayn's carefully cultivated control to stop from pulling Amalia from her boss's arms into his. This was how one of his barely civilized ancestors must have felt when their claim on their woman was challenged so blatantly.

Having always believed that a man could use his brains more effectively than fists, right now Zayn saw the appeal to the old approach.

"Amalia knows perfectly well what she means to me, Massimiliano. And I always take care of that which belongs to me."

Instead of backing off, the man frowned.

Amalia's laugh, forced and brittle, tinkled in the oppressive silence that was only punctured by the greeting called out by Parisians taking advantage of a beautiful night. Clearly, she didn't understand that men, arrogant, powerful men, used to getting their own way, communicated on a different level with each other.

Massimiliano wanted Amalia, was doing everything to show he knew her better than Zayn did. But it didn't matter.

Amalia was his, at least for now.

"Didn't I tell you meeting in secret like this is not the best idea, Massi?" Her topaz gaze flicked to him only for an instant. Finally, she moved toward him and Zayn felt a wild elation, a primal satisfaction as if he'd won a war.

She stood by him, even as every inch of her was stiff like a pole. Zayn thought she might shatter if he held her too hard. The smile that curved her lips had a tremble to it, as if she was working very hard to keep it together. "Zayn is a little too possessive."

"I'm aware of the sheik's personality, Amalia. And I've known you for five years. Which is why I find it hard to believe that you would fall for a man like him," Massi replied from behind her.

Something glittered in Amalia's eyes then, a shadow of vulnerability when she looked at him before she turned back to the Italian. "There's more to my fiancé than the world knows. And apparently, I'm no less susceptible than the next woman to a powerful sheikh's arrogant charm," she finished, her tone curiously flat.

But Zayn was far too angry to care what it meant.

All he could think of now was if she had betrayed their pact…she had reason to go to the press about their little deal; she had means through her champion to create a furor about Aslam and his release; she owed no loyalty to Zayn…

Why would she when Zayn didn't know how to inspire

trust in a woman? He knew how to charm, seduce and blackmail one...

And it wasn't Mirah's happiness that mattered to him in that moment. It was, he was shocked to discover, his own emotions that were blindsiding him from all sides.

The anger that burned through him was still coated with that fear, was not the cold ire that he kept a lid on. This was hot, fiery.

Zayn didn't know when his hand had descended to her waist, or that he was even keeping her by his side. Her body stiffened next to him, her mouth a flat line.

Slowly she undid his arm from around her, walked up to her boss and gave him a quick kiss on the cheek. "Massi, I'm with Zayn because I want to be." She said the words with conviction; still, a disquiet unfurled in Zayn's gut.

With mounting irritation, he realized he wanted Amalia to choose to be with him, to want to spend this time with him. To give in to the attraction that had been getting out of control over the past two weeks between them.

To choose him even though he was fully aware that he could give her nothing but a temporary affair.

A more ridiculous, nerve-racking thought, he'd never had.

With a start, he realized how used he'd become to seeing her face every morning over breakfast while his aide rattled off their schedule. Intermittently during the day when she played the part of his fiancée seamlessly and to utter perfection. And then at night, when she worked alongside him into the long hours without missing a beat.

That he'd begun to think of Amalia as his. He'd always been possessive about the women he slept with, demanding fidelity for as long as they were with him. With Amalia, that feeling went even deeper.

He'd become used to her irreverent humor, the paradox of cynicism and naïveté in her view of the world. Even the smile that broke through that reserve when he asked her opinion on something. Or the way she chewed her lower lip when she was either nervous or excited.

It was a relationship he'd never had with another woman, ever. Even the most time he'd spent with one—the deep understanding he was gaining of how her mind worked. That was all this fascination had to be. Had never waited to bed a woman he wanted…that was all this frustration, this restlessness in his blood, was.

Zayn Al-Ghamdi could not be losing his head, his cool, over a mere woman. But the statement sounded hollow to his ears and full of that arrogant confidence that riled her so much.

"I appreciate you looking out for me, Massi. You've always been a good friend," she finished with a soft smile. There was affection in her eyes, in her smile, when she looked at the Italian, and only a wary reserve when she turned to Zayn.

Of all the ridiculous things in the world to bother him…

"Should I consider this your resignation, then?" Massimiliano asked, his gaze locking with his over Amalia's head.

The slump in her slender shoulders twisted Zayn's gut. Did the man matter to Amalia or was it the job?

She squeezed Massimiliano's fingers. "We'll talk soon, and at length. Zayn is right. The media watches us relentlessly. I have to go."

The Italian kept his gaze on Zayn while he kissed her cheeks. "Remember you can count on me, Amalia. Against anyone and anything."

Amalia nodded, took Zayn's outstretched arm, her topaz eyes for once hiding her expression from him.

* * *

"Your knee is bleeding." Zayn's clipped words rang around the silent corridor. Amalia waited with bated breath as he slipped his key card into the door and opened it for her.

Feeling the sting in her knee now that he had pointed it out, she walked into the suite and shivered. The room was in a disarray, from papers strewn all over the room to several laptops and walkie-talkies sitting on every available surface. They had even set up a comm center in the suite, she thought, flushing with shame all over again.

It looked as if a storm had blown through the luxury suite in just a couple of hours.

"How did you hurt your knee? The rest of you—" his gaze swept over her with a thoroughness that made her insides melt "—looks fine."

"I slipped on the steps to the roof and slid down a couple of them. The side of the staircase where I banged my knee was rough." Guilt she didn't want to admit resonated in her tone. "I'm not used to heels."

His mouth hardened. "Were you in such a hurry to get away with your lover, then? Did I not offer enough of an...*inducement* for you to stay?" The taunt came before he left the room.

How could he sound so calm when it was clear he was ragingly furious? So cold, even? Her own emotions felt as if they were walking a tightrope to what, she had no idea. Amalia had never felt this turmoil, this feeling of standing at a fork not knowing which way her life was going.

When Massi had asked her to meet him on the roof, she'd given the slip to Zayn's security team. An overwhelming sense of guilt had pervaded her all the while.

As if she was really cheating on the man she was supposed to wed. As if speaking to a man who'd been her friend and confidant for so many years was turning her back on Zayn. The guilt had been a shock, driving the realization that she was far too involved in the charade.

Far too involved with Zayn...

So, instead of doing the sensible thing and informing his team, she had let that shock propel her into leaving with Massi. Even knowing that soon Zayn would note her missing and start looking for her.

Suddenly, standing in the middle of the banquet hall and catching Zayn's glance across the room, Amalia had felt as if she was losing herself, being swept along by a current that was changing her far too fast.

All she'd wanted was a short escape from the complex charade she was playing, a little touch with the reality of her life outside of being Zayn's fiancée. A desperate need to fight her own feelings.

A quick chat had turned into two hours of stubborn argument with Massi. An argument within herself for the loyalty she felt for Zayn.

It had been irresponsible, juvenile, even reckless, knowing how Zayn was going to react. It was the mixture of rage and fear that she had seen in Zayn's eyes that had brought something else from years ago to her mind.

Something similar that her mother had done, driving her father insane with worry. How she had forgotten that night, Amalia had no idea.

Any anger she had felt over his savage words had died an instantaneous death as shame filled her over her own behavior. Whatever her disagreement with him, she had no cause to have acted like a reckless wild child.

He had worried about her safety, she had realized belatedly, the white cast of his ferocious features making her guilty all over again.

Now she was sure she had made both men doubt her sanity.

She had alienated Massi, who had always been kind and fair to her, burned her bridges with the man who had helped her at the hardest time of her life. All for a man who had no use for her in his life...

God, she didn't like that she had lost all the credibility she had built up with him over the last month. Why his opinion mattered so much, she couldn't even pin that down in the chaos of her thoughts.

"Amalia, you look pale. Did you hit your head, too?"

It was her sense of self that felt bruised and battered, but she couldn't tell him that. She felt upside down, inside out, weak. "No."

The intensity of his gaze touched her, the warmth of his body a tantalizing caress. Amalia couldn't meet his gaze just yet. For some reason all her bluster and confidence seemed to have left her, leaving her shaking.

"That question didn't even get your standard outraged response. Either I'm losing my touch or something is really wrong with you."

The dry, sarcastic tone of his words didn't quite hide the anger beneath. "My head is fine. I just...I don't like the way you confronted Massi. Not his fault that I didn't tell the team where I was going."

"No, I recognize your little rebellion. But that confrontation was bound to happen the minute he decided to show up here and play knight to you."

"What does that mean?"

"Men have their own ways of communicating, especially over a woman they both want a claim on."

"That's ridicu..." Her heart slammed so hard against her rib cage that she was dizzy. "Massi does not want a *claim* on me any more than you do," she said, her voice catching in her throat dangerously.

His jaw went rigid, his expression exasperated fury.

Amalia had never felt more out of her depth than at the moment. No way to understand what it was that she felt. "Then you're truly naive in the ways of men."

Now what the hell did he mean by that? Why couldn't he just come out and say what he wanted of her?

She stretched her entire leg, and her knee stung again. With a sigh, she looked down and saw blood. For some reason her throat closed up and she felt like a leaf, ready to blow away at a small breeze. Or crunched beneath an arrogant, unfeeling man's foot.

Hand on her abdomen, she leaned against the wall, tried to make sense of the morass of feelings piling upon her.

It had been so easy, far too natural, to convince Massi that she had fallen in love with Zayn Al-Ghamdi. As the words had poured out of her mouth, conviction had set in. There was no act that she had put on for her friend's sake, no lie that she had spouted because she didn't want to betray Zayn.

She hadn't thought of Aslam or Mirah or anything else.

Only the glitter in Zayn's eyes when he had provoked her, the charming smile that softened his mouth when they argued, the touch of his hand at the base of her spine that made her want to melt into him...

She had fallen in love with Sheikh Zayn Al-Ghamdi of Khaleej. If her mother's love for her father had been a mistake, Amalia's was a blunder of epic proportions.

They had spent two weeks under the same roof, working and talking and arguing and yet, today, the intimacy of their shared suite seemed to scrape her raw.

"There's a first-aid box in my bathroom," she said, not meeting his gaze. She wanted to escape his dark glare and examine her newfound feelings in the privacy of her bedroom. "I'll take care of it. Good night, Zayn."

"Sit down on that chaise." He ordered her around as if she were three years old.

Finally, it sparked her temper again. "I'm not a child."

"Then stop cowering like one. I've never hit a woman before, however furious she might make me. No, that's not true. I've never met a woman who made me this furious and worried, and I've known a few women in my life."

The last thing she wanted was to hear about the women in his life.

She pushed off from the wall, intending to reach her room come what may. "I said I'll take care of—"

In one sweeping movement, Zayn picked her up.

Amalia gasped.

His long fingers pressed into her rib cage, the knuckles grazing the underside of her breast and she lost all the will to fight in one swooping breath. His shoulders were like a wall of steel under her arm, his mouth unyielding and harsh, like the desert land of his ancestors.

Not his, *their*, ancestors. For the first time in her life, Amalia wanted to own her heritage, to belong to the same world that had made this man.

Of all the men in the world, how had she fallen for this hard, aloof man? A man who had ruthlessly decided that he would naturally take a mistress after he had sons. A man who decided that he could not open himself even to his wife.

Much as she would've preferred it otherwise, she had fallen in love with the sheikh, and Amalia knew she couldn't have just the man, Zayn.

Her fingers tightened around his nape; she hid her face in his chest. The scent of him filled her nostrils, the warmth of the man twisting the longing in her chest tighter.

The depth of her need frightened her.

He deposited her with a surprising gentleness that belied the dark scowl on his face, on the chaise longue. "If you value your independence, Amalia, you will not use that tart tongue on me today."

"Or what, you'll lock me up and ship me back to Khaleej like a disgrace? Build that jail cell for me next to Aslam's?"

Hands on his lean hips, he towered over her. Since he'd marched onto the roof, Amalia looked at him properly for the first time. Deep grooves settled on the sides of his mouth, and her heart ached.

All six foot four inches of muscle and aggression and forceful will towered over her, his battle to keep his temper under control clear in his tight mouth. And instead of being angry or afraid, her heart pumped faster, her blood sang.

Passion, she wanted his passion, too…

Just then, he hadn't sounded in control. She'd never seen him in such a dangerous mood. Was he still worried about her because he counted himself responsible for her? Or was that emotion in his tone more personal?

Before she could get her muddled thoughts under control, he returned with the first-aid box. Her breath knocked into her throat when he knelt at her feet and pulled her leg onto his muscled thigh. His black trousers pulled up, delineating the hard strength of his thighs.

She jerked at the clench of his muscle under her foot, at the sensations pouring through her at that simple contact. Hurriedly, she shuffled her toes away from reaching up toward his groin. "Zayn, I can manage this."

Thick black hair gleamed, her fingers tingling to run through it. To learn every inch of his hard body, to share an intimacy she'd never wanted before. "For both our sakes, I suggest you put away that headstrong, stubborn independence of yours for the night, Amalia. You will not find me manageable like the other men you—"

"*Suggest?* You never suggest. You command, order…

you… And just because Massi respects my opinion does not mean he's less of a man than you are, you arrogant ass."

He looked up then, a ferocious blaze in his golden-brown eyes. But instead of calling her mouth tart, or her attitude offensive, he said, "I am what I have to be, Amalia. I will never be a sensitive or a tender man, neither will I act civilized when the woman I want sneaks away to be in another man's arms."

And just like that, he stole away the ground from under her. And the breath from her lungs. And the last of her will from her.

With gentle fingers that belied his explosive mood, he pulled the offending four-inch heel off her foot. "Why do you wear them if you're not used to them? You're tall enough for me without heels anyway."

"Not everything I do or wear is to make myself perfect for you," she threw at him, fighting the little burst of pleasure in her chest.

When his fingers lifted the hem of her dress higher above her knees, Amalia froze. "What are you doing? Don't…lift my dress like that."

The broad line of his shoulders tensed. "Move forward and roll your pantyhose down slowly. The blood's already crusted and it's going to sting."

She reached for the hem of her dress and then looked at Zayn. Her breath came hard and shallow, coated with the scent of him. "Turn around."

The very devil lurked in his eyes. "I have seen women's legs and more before."

"You have not seen mine." No man had seen hers.

His head cocked, the sinful curve of his mouth a dare. "I have noticed that they go on and on and have had dreams about them. Especially how they would look and feel wrapped around my hips while I—"

Amalia rocked forward, her entire body shuddering with heat. "Please... Zayn."

Long fingers reached up to her cheek and stroked. "You're really that shy." He stated it with the confidence of a man who had known her for years. "I have not met a beautiful woman who did not know her worth or who didn't take complete advantage of her looks."

"I was taught the opposite. My mother pleaded with me relentlessly not to make much of my beauty, to make sure I found a man who didn't think of owning me as much as he loved me... That in her case, it had turned out to be a curse that attracted the wrong kind of man. She..."

He tugged her hand into his. "Amalia, you know that—"

"I know," she whispered back. "She loved me, Zayn, and she wanted me to be happy. But yes, I realize now that she probably lost all objectivity when it came to men and matters of love. But you see, I started working as soon as possible. I neither had the time nor the energy for a social life, and Massi and my mom ended up being the total of my world."

A tightness descended on his face, a dark glitter in his eyes. He looked dangerous, almost savage. "I do not want to talk about Massi anymore." His thumb traced the plump vein on her wrist. "At some point you have to move out of her shadow and begin living, Amalia."

He stood up and went to the small kitchenette the suite had while she wiggled her hands under her dress and started pulling the sheer material down.

Just as he had predicted, the material clung to her cut when it came to her knees. A small gasp fell from her mouth. Again, Zayn appeared at her knees, put one large hand on her thigh and tugged with the other hand hard.

The material came away with a tearing sound and Amalia felt the prickle of tears. She bent her head while Zayn pulled the tights all the way down. Then with gentle fingers, he cleaned the cut, dabbed antiseptic cream on.

His arrogant head bent over her in concern, a rush of emotions surged through Amalia. The gash had been pretty small in the scheme of things but it had been so long since someone had looked after her with such thoroughness. Not since she had gone to live with her mother.

It was as if that small act of tenderness had unlocked a memory she had completely blocked out.

Her father had always been protective of her, even as he'd encouraged her to be more playful and Aslam, who was the opposite to her in temperament, to employ more caution.

Overnight, Amalia had become the stable one, the parent in the relationship. She'd buried the hurt over how easily her father had abandoned her; the ache she felt to be with Aslam again erected a shell around herself so that she could move forward.

Had she stopped living that day, too?

No, she'd done that later, after seeing her mother grieve day after day, pine over her father year after year. Hardened herself so much that she'd refused to even talk to her father when Aslam nudged her. She'd done nothing that could hurt her like that, taken no chances.

But something inside her roared, *If not now, when? When would she live? Was she willing to give up this time with Zayn, knowing that she might never have another such chance?*

At that moment Amalia couldn't care less if he was right for her or not, or that he was exactly the kind of man she'd sworn she'd never fall for…or that when these few months were over, and he had no use for this charade or her, he would simply remove her from his life…or the worst, that he would just go back to his damn Ms. Young and those candidates for his brides…no future with him.

All she wanted was to feel his touch, to feel like the woman she was supposed to be, to live her life away from the shadow of her mother's own love story.

When he tried to rise, she stopped him with her hands on his shoulders. Pulling in a much-needed breath, she stole her fingers under the collar of his shirt, searching for skin.

The tendons in his neck stuck out.

His skin was like rough silk, so warm that it sent a pulse of heat straight to the core of her. How would it feel if he was naked on top of her against her own bare skin, all that fierce power and passion narrowed down to her. A pulse throbbed between her thighs, bringing fresh heat to her cheeks.

The line of his shoulders was hard, tense. He said, "I see that seeing Massi has made you emotional and perhaps nostalgic, but if you provoke me tonight, I—"

Amalia leaned forward until her face was bent over his. Fingers trembling, she pushed a lock of hair that fell forward onto his forehead. Traced the strong, proud planes of his face. The sharp hiss of his breath was the only sound. "Among those women Ms. Young sent you that day, did you pick one?"

Warning glittered in his dark eyes. "That's the last thing I want to talk about right now."

Her fingers crept under his collar again, roaming and searching, her body articulating her need before her mind could. "No, I want to know." She tried to speak past the closing of her throat. "Is there a candidate in your mind, one you decided will suit you perfectly once you dispose of me and my...situation."

"No," he said, his fingers pushing through his hair in a restless gesture she'd never seen in him. Their fingers tangled and laced, his grip fierce. "Even for the schedule

I have, I cannot just dump you and go to the next woman on the list. Right now all I care about is making sure you… Mirah weds Farid. After that…" His mouth twitched as if they were co-conspirators. "Your blackmail scheme bought me a little time. I am sure even my staunchest opponent in the cabinet and conservatives in Sintar would not expect that I marry soon after one engagement is broken."

Her breath left her in a soft exhale. As long as he hadn't given a woman a role in his life, he was hers.

And she would make most of this time with the man she loved, this opportunity at hand. She would not waste her life like her mom had done.

Anticipation and excitement twined together inside her, making her voice husky, uneven. "Zayn, will you make love to me?"

CHAPTER NINE

WILL YOU MAKE love to me?

Even as he stood under the cold shower jets, Zayn couldn't get those words out of his mind, nor get his X-rated thoughts and body to cool off.

It was the last thing he'd expected Amalia to say tonight. A taunt on his lips, he'd looked up and read the resolve in her eyes.

She wanted him.

All his life, he had surrounded himself with brazen, sophisticated women who wanted sex and mutual pleasure or women like his third PA and the candidates sent over by Ms. Young, who only saw the glitter and power of his position in the world.

Amalia fell into neither camp and yet, to both. From the time he could understand the world he'd been told that he was the prince, the future sheikh, not just Zayn. Never just Zayn.

And yet he felt different, both and neither when held by her alluring gaze, when she glared at him or argued with him even.

With a gritted jaw, he realized she might not be truly innocent, but it was clear that she was inexperienced. A woman he'd begun to understand and admire. A woman he couldn't blithely seduce and walk away from when the curtain fell on their charade.

Damn it, she had looked crushed when he'd claimed he needed a shower and left the room without acknowledging her question. As if it wasn't the hardest thing he'd ever done in his life—to walk away from the lush temptation she presented.

He stepped out of the shower and toweled himself dry.

Sharing the suite with Amalia for the duration of their stay in Paris seemed to be the worst idea he had ever had. Right in line with choosing to keep her close by parading her as his fiancée.

Knowing that she was in the next room, probably freshly showered like he was…just the passing thought sent a flurry of images through his overheated mind.

Her silky skin would be soft and damp, the towel sticking to those pouty breasts that had finally been displayed in their full glory in that dress tonight. Her long, toned legs would be bare under the towel, would be perfect wrapped around his waist as he…

Gritting his jaw, he wrapped the towel against his hips and walked out into his bedroom. The Paris skyline was a feast outside the French windows but tonight he drew no pleasure from it.

The jar of the door behind him made every muscle curl with heat and want.

He turned to find her leaning against the closed door. Her hands hung limply by her sides. A fine tension seemed to resonate from her but it was her face that arrested him.

Her face was free of even the little makeup she had worn earlier. Hair tied up in that ponytail again, pulled tautly from her forehead. She wore a knee-length robe tightly cinched at her waist.

And just as he guessed, her legs went on and on under the hem, tanned and shapely in the moonlight. Seeing a woman's bare legs for the first time had never been such an intimate act. A small gold chain hung at her neck where her pulse pounded violently, quite like his heart inside his chest.

"You're probably used to and expect all sorts of flimsy, sheer stuff—" pink scoured her cheeks here "—but I don't have any…sex clothes," she finished, and absurdly, he wanted to laugh.

She didn't wait for his answer, either. Pushing away from the door, she glanced around the room. On every third breath of his, her gaze focused back on him and then skittered away quite without landing. She halted when she came to the middle of the room, her bare toes pressing into the thick carpet.

"Amalia, I did not—"

"Lisa…the stylist, did ask me if I wanted to look at some lingerie and nightgowns, too, and I was like, *dude*… the last thing I'm going to do on this trip is have sex and she gave me this strange look, I mean, I didn't actually say it…anyway, so I only chose a couple of cute pajama sets."

She undid the sash of her silky robe and shrugged her shoulders to let it slide off.

The robe pooled at her feet and Zayn's breath slammed into his throat.

Somehow he possessed enough wits still to say, "I would not call that attire cute."

She scrunched her nose and he had the most overwhelming urge to kiss the stubborn tip of it. He had been seduced before, yes, but it had been a game he had willingly played.

This…*whatever* it was that Amalia was doing, it disarmed him on more levels than he could fathom. Resolve and innocence played in her every word, every action. Never had a woman beguiled him so thoroughly…

Navy blue silk top with thin straps bared pale skin and fluttered against her breasts. His mouth dry, he watched as her nipples pointed against the silk. He would tongue them and suck them into his mouth; he would make sure she'd never forget about him. The top left a strip of flesh at her midriff bare while her shorts barely covered her toned thighs.

He cleared his throat, his blood rushing sluggishly through every nerve ending now. "I cannot offer you anything beyond the next couple of months." Hands fisted by his sides, he saw that made no dent in the resolve in her eyes. His will against hers—tonight, Zayn realized, he was going to lose. "It is why I have been trying my best to not indulge in all the fantasies I have of you every night."

She swallowed and nodded. Every second seemed to stretch between them while his heart pounded. "You've had fantasies about me?" An edge of complaint crept into her tone. "All these days, I've been wondering, going crazy…"

"I did not think—" his skin felt tightly stretched over his hungry muscles "—it a good idea for you to know the power you could have over me."

Her face fell. "That's what this will be, too, between us, Zayn? A power struggle? An agreement?"

"No, but why tonight, Amalia? I will not be a replacement for another man."

Her head jerked up, and the breath bated in his throat. "I don't want Massi. I've never felt this way about him or any other man." The flutter of a breeze played with the hem of her top, giving him a peek of silky soft flesh and the cute indentation of her navel. Every silky inch of her— he would learn it, lick it, know it. "You were right. I have to start living my own life now and this…you and I, this is what I want."

The urge to fasten his mouth at the pulse on her neck and taste the small drop of water clinging there rode him hard. She licked that pillowy lower lip and all the blood in his body fled south. "Yet, your gaze will not land on me."

Finally, she met his gaze. Resolve laced with naked desire in her eyes razed the last bit of reason from his mind. "Put your hair down," he demanded in a rough tone, a sense of defeat in his veins making his voice harsh.

Was it defeat just because he was indulging himself? Because the lines between his private and public life were blurring?

He'd been given a respite from the marriage he had to make, so why not take it? Why shouldn't he, for once in his life, have a meaningful, if brief, relationship with a woman he admired? A woman who incited more than just lust in him?

"What?" she asked, face blazing, long lashes barely revealing her expression.

"*Your hair*…it is always tied up like that or hidden away in some elaborate style."

"It took me two hours to get it into this style," she complained.

The return of her backbone made him smile. "I hate it like that. I want to see it down." He could practically feel those silky strands wound up around his fingers as he held her still beneath him. While he plundered her mouth and filled her body.

Fever took root in his muscles. But he held the words to himself. The last thing he wanted was to scare or hurt her when she'd come to him with such artless desire.

Amalia wasn't like any other woman he bedded and not just because she was inexperienced. She was someone who should be cherished and loved and cared for. Loyal to the last, with a steely core, and beautiful on the outside and inside, such a woman deserved a man who would worship her. Not use her in a torrid affair under a pretend engagement…

But all the recriminations in the world were not going to make him turn back on tonight. There was one thing he could make sure Amalia had tonight and he would give her that—pleasure.

She set those doe eyes on him for so long that he thought she would protest. Desire clashed with anticipation inside him while he waited. Slowly, she raised her hands and tugged the band holding the tousled waves. Just as that day on the flight, the movement thrust her breasts up, and his belly tightened.

Hair that was the color of burnished gold fell down in lustrous waves, framing the delicate angles of her face. She pushed her hand into it and shook it out, an intrinsically feminine action that made his mouth dry. It fell to her waist and to her midriff in the front, covering the outline of her nipples from him.

Suddenly, the custom that the Bedouins followed, making their women cover their hair except in front of their men, seemed a very good idea. Magnificent and lustrous, he wanted no other man to see her like that…no other man to know how she would look with only her hair hiding her body from his eyes…

"It's too much to manage and takes almost an hour to wash and dry. I'm going to ask the stylist to cut off most of it. Maybe something really short and fun now that I—"

"No." His voice hadn't risen but the command in it carried around the room.

Her fingers stilled in the silky weight, her eyes wide in her face. "No what?"

"Do not cut it. And that's an order."

She laughed then, and the defiance in her eyes greeted him like an old friend.

"I mean it, Amalia. Cutting it off would be a crime."

"Zayn, you can't order me to... I want to be your lover, not your...your..."

He raised a brow and waited, his mouth twitching. "When you look at my body, which I know you've been avoiding since you entered the room, does it give you pleasure, *habibti*?"

Those long eyelashes lifted and her gaze did a sweep of his torso. Slowly and thoroughly over his naked chest and abdomen, flitted sideways to his lean hips and the towel resting there. Then stopped at the line of hair that disappeared beneath his towel.

"I don't see all of you, Sheikh," the minx demanded then, and husky laughter came from his chest. Her hand moved to her nape, a restless slither of her body that made his skin stretch taut all over him. "Drop that towel and I can tell you whether you please me or not."

He raised a brow at her saucy tone. No woman had ordered him like she did, nor demanded her due.

Chewing her lower lip between her teeth, she looked up. "What? I can't order...I mean ask my lover to—"

He dropped the towel. The air was a cool whisper against his heated skin.

Her mouth opened and a soft gasp slid out of those lush lips. That pink mouth wrapped around the head, that tongue licking the length of him...images tightened his body to near torturous arousal.

"Does my fiancée find me to her liking?"

Color made her sharp cheekbones even more pronounced. Her breath left her in a whistle, breasts rising and falling. Her hand drifted to her abdomen and Zayn smiled at how telling her gestures were. At how artlessly naive she was even when she taunted with her words.

"I wouldn't be a woman if I didn't like the look of you,

I think." She swallowed as he took a step toward her. "And I completely forgot where we were going with this."

He pulled long strands of her silky hair and wound it around his fingers, tugging her closer and closer. She came with her mouth upturned, her body thrumming lightly. "Your hair…" He traced the lush lips. "Everything about your body drives me crazy even when you hide most of it. I wouldn't want to lose that pleasure. Just as you wouldn't want me right now to cover up, yes?"

"My pleasure feeds yours and yours mine," she whispered, her words throaty.

"Yes."

She covered the last few steps between them. Hands on her shoulders, Zayn pulled her closer until the silk of her top rasped against his body. Her forehead fell against his chest, her body shaking.

"You're trembling. I would never hurt you."

Not physically, she knew. But what about her heart?

Amalia lifted her face to Zayn's and lost the ability to breathe all over again. Such a breathtaking face rendered harsh by his will, implacable by his duty…and all she could see in that moment was the desire that unfurled in it, for her.

How had she doubted whether he wanted her?

She felt as if she was suspended over a cloud of desire and need, not quite able to land her feet anywhere. As if there were a rope that was hooked into her lower belly tugging her higher and higher, amplifying every sense…

The dark gleam of desire in his eyes prodding her, she touched her lips to his. Instant heat sizzled over them as lips merged with lips, as her breasts rubbed against his hard chest. Groans rippled through the charged air, erotic sounds full of need and desperation that played over her nerves.

He took over the kiss almost instantly, none of that gentling in his caress now as that first kiss. Such harshly contoured lips could kiss so softly.

"You taste like a berry, Amalia, tart and sweet, incredibly erotic. And I'm going to taste you everywhere…"

She groaned as his legs spread and created a cradle for her own. The contrast of his body against hers sent ripple after ripple of sensation over her. They were so different in so many ways and yet it seemed their bodies were made for this, every press of their muscles, every whispered slither of skin against skin ramping up the need.

Clutching his nape, Amalia sank her fingers into his thick hair and pressed herself to him. The jut of his manhood against her lower belly, thick and hot, branded her.

Fingers held her jaw tight while he plundered her mouth. His lips devoured her upper lip, the erotic swipe of his tongue teasing her to do the same. But when she did, he backed off. Until she demurred and he started all over again.

In minutes her lips felt swollen, hot, her breasts were crushed against his hard chest, her lungs burning to keep up with her heart.

This kiss was one of possession, of primal masculinity demanding her surrender, of the wild desert heat finally claiming her for his own.

She surrendered willingly, slapping her fingers onto his bare chest.

His muscles clenched under her fingers, the fine hairs on his chest tickling her palms. Golden tanned skin stretched taut over pectorals that were defined but lean.

His tongue delved into her mouth while his hands landed on her hips. Amalia shuddered all over as his tongue called hers into a wildly erotic dance that made her toes curl into the carpet at her feet.

Oh, the press of his arousal against her lower belly…an answering ache spread low within.

When he pushed his hand under her top and branded her hot flesh with his fingers, she wanted to do the same. Her questing touch roved over his hard chest hungrily and soon she discovered that she affected him just as he did her.

Hot mouth skimmed over her jaw, the sensitive rim of her ear and then the pulse at her neck…when he dug his teeth into her skin, Amalia jerked in his arms, a jolt of heat narrowing down to her core.

So many sensitized places throbbed under his expert caresses; so many sensations battered at her that she felt her breath saw in and out of her in an unsteady rhythm.

But even under the assault, a dim sort of doubt lingered at the back of her mind. He'd done this so many times with so many women. Even if she didn't believe all the numbers that exposé had quoted, his expert caresses, the way he'd already learned how he could play her body, how to turn her on so skillfully, it spoke of what an experienced lover he was. God, already he knew her body better than she herself did.

Amalia didn't want to be another woman the playboy sheikh took to his bed to satisfy his voracious appetite. A convenient relief after the hard, relentless pressures of the last two weeks. "Zayn…" She pulled his face down to hers, breathing so hard that the sound echoed in the thick air.

His hard chest rose and fell, his hands pulling her hips flush against his.

"You didn't ask me if I betrayed our deal to Massi."

Sensuous lips pulled back to a snarl. "You're asking me this now? Now? Amalia, if your plan is to—"

"How do you know I haven't?"

Nimble fingers crawled up and up her abdomen under her top, and cupped her breasts. His fingers were abrasive, rough against her sensitive skin. A working man's hands… And then he covered the hard nubs with his palms, kneading and lifting one to his mouth.

Something harsh fell from his mouth in Arabic. In the haze of desire, she couldn't catch what it was. Every inch of her trembling, she stared as he lifted the pouty nipple to his mouth and flicked it through her top. A bolt of pure desire shot through her and Amalia arched her body into his, a pit of longing in her gut.

"Seeing you in his arms made me forget everything, *azeezi*. About Sintar, about my duty, about Mirah's happiness, about your brother and the media… I forgot everything." He punctured the words with flicks of his tongue and now he took the nipple into his mouth and sucked it. Amalia pinched her thighs together against the arrows of pleasure converging around her sex. "So you tell me now. Have you betrayed our deal, Amalia?"

She sobbed when he released her nipple with a soft plop, her entire being tense like a bow. With hands that could play her like a violin, he took the hem of her top and pulled it up over her head until her torso was bare to him.

And then his hands stroked over the flesh he had uncovered. Large hands pressed and stroked her until all she could do was give herself over. Moving to her shoulders, he kneaded her back, so aggressively male that Amalia drowned in him.

"Did you, *ya habibti*? Did seeing Massi remind you what an arrogant beast I was in comparison?"

Amalia didn't want to agree. She wanted to remind him of his tenderness when he'd thought she'd hurt herself, the concern she'd read in his eyes because he'd feared for her safety. But no sooner than the thought formed, he drove it out with his fingers plucking restlessly at her turgid nipples.

Hardly had she shaken her head before he resumed the plunder of his mouth on her other breast.

Again and again, he ministered to her breasts until the wet points were tender and sensitized, until a fever ran in her blood. Pain and pleasure seemed to coalesce and beat like one pulse all through her body.

When he stopped his caresses and moved his hands down her body, Amalia felt like her entire body was waiting for a breath, parched. Like she'd been waiting her entire life for this moment with this man. The pulse he had built to a keening pitch between her thighs dulled down. And she was desperate enough to beg. "Please, Zayn, I need—"

"Not yet, *habibti*." Dry amusement sprinkled his words. "First, I shall make sure you are ready for me, yes?"

Amalia protested with a sob. He was already holding her up, her quivering legs of no use. A hand under her knee urged it up and she locked it around his hip. The graze of his hip bone, the rough musculature against her inner thigh, sent a moan hurtling through her, the press of his shaft against the core of her sending an ache through it.

She hid her face in his chest at the way he opened up the heart of her, heat flooding her cheeks. "Zayn, that's… the bed…"

A wicked gleam in his eyes, he pressed a sizzling kiss to her damp mouth. "No, here," he whispered, before his fingers found the wet heat of her.

Amalia groaned as he pushed one, then two fingers into her core, while his thumb pressed and stroked the spot that ached for his touch.

His jaw gritted so tight to resemble a marble cast, he looked down at her. Passion pinched his features, all the hard contours of his face even more pronounced now. "You're swollen and wet for me, Amalia." When he tweaked the bud with his fingers, Amalia jerked at the wave of pleasure that claimed her. "And so violently responsive. Shall I take you like this, *latifa*?"

Amalia knew she should say something but the sight of his leanly powerful body arrested her words. While she watched with widening eyes and whistling breath, he ripped off the cover on a condom and rolled it on.

Her mouth went dry. She went willingly when he took her in his arms again and his fingers plunged into her wet core as if they belonged there. The insistent pressure and strokes of his fingers sent wave after wave of such blinding pleasure that she clung to him to ride each.

She was so close, so desperate for that peak, she dug her teeth into his flesh and panted against his skin.

In the next breath, he was lifting her as if she was a petite, fragile thing, urging her to wrap her legs around his hips. The wall kissed her bare spine, while his muscles pressed into her front. His fingers left her just as Amalia hung on the edge of her climax and then he was entering her with one hard thrust…

Stinging pain rippled through her core and Amalia tried to contain her whimper against one rock-hard shoulder. And failed. Every inch of her went rigid against the waves of pain.

This time she understood the curse words that fell from his mouth.

His fingers gentled on her hips, his breathing like bellows around her. "Damn it, Amalia…why didn't you tell me?" He sounded so utterly pained that she lifted her head and looked at him.

Such tender concern filled his gaze that the fingers of pain dulled by a deeper longing. "I should have, I know. But I did tell you that I haven't had much life beyond my mother and Massi…" Her words drifted off as she saw his jaw tighten. "You thought I had been with Massi?"

"Yes. It was clear in his eyes that he wanted more, Amalia."

"He did. We tried a couple of dates but I couldn't…I just couldn't see him as anything other than my boss. And maybe an older brother. So I told him that I didn't want to ruin what we had."

"It is clear from his gaze today that he still…" He stopped and carried her to the vast bed. He brought her to the edge of it and gently lowered her. He'd already pulled out of her and all she felt was an aching awareness, a void in her sex, just like the one in her chest.

God, she didn't want the night to end yet, not like this.

Fingers tight against his biceps, she stayed him. Pressed her face to his chest and breathed in the musky scent of him. His skin was smooth and rough at the same time, a damp sheen clinging to it. "Don't leave me, Zayn… I came to you tonight because I wanted this."

He clasped her cheek gently, his eyes full of a warmth that set her heart racing. "Hurting you physically is bad enough, Amalia. I can't justify—"

"But it is a pain I welcomed willingly," she pleaded, beyond pride or shame now.

Gentle fingers dug into her hair, molding the shape of her head. She'd never seen the conflict mirrored in his eyes as she did now. Something expanded in her chest, as if this fight he was going through between what he was supposed to be and what he wanted was a personal victory of hers. As if she had smashed through to the complex man beneath. "You know where my life is headed. If you waited this long, it should have been with someone special. I just—"

"You're special to me, Zayn." Instantly, his gaze shuttered and Amalia reached up to touch his face. "No, please don't…withdraw from me. I'm not asking for anything. I do feel…there is a connection between us, do you deny it?"

"It's attraction, Amalia. Lust at its most primal."

She swallowed away the hurt that pinched at his dismissal. "Well, you're the first man I've lusted over quite like this. So…how about you make good on your promise,

Sheikh?" She filled her tone with taunt, desperate to have him finish what he started, desperate to have that closeness with him again. "Shouldn't I get some reward for the pain I just felt? Or are you in the habit of leaving your woman unsatisfied? I wonder if that tabloid—"

"You're a stubborn, manipulative witch," he mumbled while he climbed over her onto the bed. Amalia slid up the sheets, her breath stuttering in her throat again.

His golden skin tautly stretched over a gorgeously hard body, Zayn took her breath away. He rested alongside her, his hands palms down on her body, restlessly stroking her everywhere.

Amalia closed her eyes and arched into his touch when he strummed her breasts again. Caught between the cool silk of the sheets and the heat of his knowing touches, she drowned in sensations. This time she was a little more aware of her own body's partiality and she gave in to the delirious pull at her sex.

Then she felt his mouth at her nipples, suckling and stroking, while her body climbed higher and higher. When his other hand rested on her mound again, she tensed, the reminder of that cleaving pain driving her reaction.

He kissed the upper curve of her breast, "Shh...*habibti*, just relax. You trust me, don't you, Amalia?"

Amalia opened her eyes and fell deep into his molten gaze. Her lips sought his and she moaned at how familiarly exciting he already was to her. How every inch of her recognized and thrummed for him. "I do."

"Then give yourself over, hmm?" His fingers delved into her folds again and resumed stroking her.

Amalia brought her knees up and held his shoulders as he increased the pressure. Faster and faster while his mouth tugged her nipple again. She was panting, flying, every inch of her being concentrated on the pulls of her sex. The hunger was so intense that she felt like weeping for release.

"You're a firecracker. Just listen to your body, *latifa*, and demand what you want from me," Zayn whispered in a barely recognizable husky tone. She heard the smile in his words instead of seeing it. "Like you always do."

As if that was all her body needed, she rocked into his touch, raising her hips, her fingers desperately holding on to his hard body. "Faster, Zayn, now," she demanded wantonly and had the pleasure of hearing his deep laughter. The soft graze of his teeth against the tautly aching nipple sent Amalia soaring over the edge.

Pleasure splintered and shattered her into a thousand flashes of light and even before the tremors subsided, he thrust into her in one smooth, deep stroke. The groan that fell from his mouth was drawn out, rubbing against her senses. Amplified the utter sense of completion she felt down to her bones.

Pain this time was more of a fading imprint. Utterly replete, Amalia opened her eyes as his hands held her shoulders and he settled so deeply into her that she didn't know where she ended and he began.

She ran her hands all over his hard body. His muscles clenched under her touch, a fine sheen of sweat covering his smooth skin.

"You feel incredibly good, *habibti*. I won't last long."

She loved seeing the dark desire in his eyes, the unraveling self-control. In that moment he was hers, Amalia knew. The sated languor left her body as he flipped her in a blink.

Every nerve ending felt tautly stretched as he pulled his legs forward and they were facing each other—nose to nose, lips to lips, and hips to hips. "Now, let's see if we can make you scream again," he whispered, sucking the tender flesh at her neck.

Such greedy languor spread through her lower belly that Amalia instinctively rose from his grip and then pushed herself back on him.

This time it was he who growled, his flesh pleading with her to not leave him. "Ride me, Amalia. I'm yours," he said, and it was all the encouragement she needed.

She gloried in grinding herself against him, again and again, up and down until a bone-deep pleasure spread its fingers through her sex again.

When he thrust up, a wave of such piercing pleasure splintered through her that she screamed. And then she was landing on her back again, his big body covering hers as he thrust sharper and faster, exploding her pleasure into a newer level. Amalia locked her ankles around his, urging him on shamelessly, the move as instinctual as breathing.

He took her mouth in a hard, punishing kiss as his body bucked above hers and he climaxed with a guttural growl. And his bellowing breath fell around her, and his sweat-kissed body folded over her almost crushing breath. Amalia wrapped her arms around his sinewy strength and held on.

She felt like she was reborn, renewed, part of which was the raw experience of being possessed by this arrogant man. But part of it was this amazement at herself, too, for taking a chance with him, for taking a risk with her heart.

As her breath softened and her body felt boneless, fear touched that euphoria, too. She kissed his damp shoulder, her fingers tightening around him.

Because sharing this intimacy, opening her body to him, would make it a thousand times harder when it was time to leave him. But if she was given a choice as to knowing this with Zayn and a pain-free life, she knew she would make this choice again and again.

CHAPTER TEN

"Your fiancée is both beautiful and smart, Your Highness." Translation: "Did you know that she is one of those modern, independent women?"

"Your fiancée has some interesting opinions about our education reforms, Your Highness." Which actually translated to "This woman of yours thinks far too much. Control her."

"Your fiancée, Zayn, has some strange ideas about Khaleej. Tell her where her place is before she becomes a liability." This glittering warning from his father while his gaze held Zayn's in a question.

A man who didn't mince words, his advice was, "She's a PA, Zayn. You could still keep her on in whatever position you want, and marry a suitable woman."

Zayn had walked away before he could give voice to the storm brewing within him, before he forgot that this man was his father, a man who always deserved Zayn's respect and loyalty.

The thought of making Amalia his mistress while he married another, reducing their relationship to that dimension, filled him with bile. Why when he had always accepted it as part of his fate? Was a faceless woman in the future in the same role just more palatable than a woman with whom he had shared the deepest and truest parts of himself?

For that was her appeal. With Amalia, he need not be just the sheikh or just Zayn. There was no dichotomy inside himself. He could be both and neither and still be comfortable in his skin, still know that he could trust in her absolutely.

Know that she understood everything that drove him, that made him who he was.

That kind of intimacy where they learned of each other, where they realized that there was so much more to learn, was both terrifying and exciting.

And addictively immersive.

The warnings and innuendos landed on Zayn like a pelt of stones, jarring the dreamy, drugged haze he seemed to be existing in in the month since their return from Paris, stirring inside him a violent urge to pound his fists into the nearest wall.

But since he hadn't given in to that urge when he had been thirteen and his father had had his secretary transferred because the man's fourteen-year-old son, who had been Zayn's first, and probably only, best friend, was being a disrupting, corruptive influence on the prince, he didn't do it now.

He pressed a hand to the back of his head where a soft pounding was beginning and retreated to a table at the corner of the hall. The way he was feeling right now, he would probably bite the head off some poor staff member who didn't deserve his wrath. And the ones who did, the one who spoke of Amalia as if she was somehow beneath them, he could not shower his displeasure.

Signaling a passing waiter for some coffee, Zayn leaned back in his seat and closed his eyes. The fragrance of coffee that wafted toward his nostrils lightened the growing tightness he was beginning to recognize in his chest.

He picked up his cup and took a sip. Amalia had gone from complaining that the brew was too bitter and pouring coffee into the creamer than the other way, to now asking what she had to do to ensure he sent her a supply of coffee for the rest of her life when she left Khaleej.

Even as he had been beyond tempted to voice his darkest desire, he had known that it was also a reminder. A reminder that she wasn't forgetting that this was only an arrangement between them, that she knew the status quo.

That she didn't, and never would, expect more of him than he was willing to give. That she wouldn't get emotional and clingy when it was time to leave.

She gave so willingly and wantonly of herself to him in the dark of the night but Amalia also prided herself on her self-respect. She wouldn't venture where she wasn't sure of her welcome, her stubborn will her shield in so many ways.

Look how they'd been in Sintar for a month and she refused to still visit her father. Zayn knew from his aide that Professor Hadid had called her numerous times. He had even come to the palace but she bluntly refused to see him. Put him off with some excuse.

"Now he worries about where all this will end and what damage I might do to his reputation," she had said when Zayn had argued that Professor Hadid was obviously concerned.

Amalia's tough attitude hid so much hurt. Confronting her father, he knew, would break her. A vulnerable, hurting Amalia, he also knew, could become his own kryptonite.

So he let it be, even as he knew she had to face her father sooner or later.

Looking out around the vast hall where Mirah's fiancé's

family was mingling with his own relatives, he pulled in a deep breath. He needed to shake off this spiraling feeling of losing his control, of being caught in an eddy.

Everything was going according to his own plan, he reminded himself. The risk he had taken with Amalia had paid off. Even as they questioned his choice, no one had doubted his relationship with Amalia.

The palace was ringing with the groom's family and the wedding guests enjoying the lavish three-day celebrations that preceded the wedding. Even after this breakfast there were ceremonial events he had to attend as the bride's brother and the sheikh.

Mirah's *nikah* to Farid was tomorrow night and that was all that mattered, at least, for now. Not he nor Amalia or their all too real-feeling relationship.

He didn't know why the shock and taunts of his friends and guests, even his parents, was leaving such a bad taste in his mouth. It was not news to him what Amalia was or what kind of a reaction she would draw from people who called themselves his well-wishers.

All he wanted to point out was that she had been by his side constantly for six weeks now and all she'd done was carry herself out in public with grace and decorum that made her no less than any daughter of some distinguished royal house that were assembled at the wedding even now.

Even when she disagreed with people's views or faced prejudice just because she was a woman and an outsider, she did it with logic and conviction, with respect, even when she was denied it.

He also hadn't failed to notice that she had ruffled more than one conservative cabinet's feathers, and didn't limit herself to a vapid, social existence. Even in the pretense, she had already involved herself in more than a few social issues and charity boards.

It was whiplash, for his statesmen had never seen a woman get involved in so many things, never mind break so many unwritten rules.

He had just finished his coffee when he heard a wave of excitement at the entrance to the hall. Dressed in a pale cream long-sleeved dress made of the sheerest silk and lace and with thousands of dollars' worth of beadwork, Mirah walked into the hall. And next to her, dressed in a light mint-green dress was his fiancée.

Sheer sleeves covered her long arms, while lace panels covered her chest and neck. Demure and stylish, and yet utterly sensuous, she took his breath away. She smiled at female members of the groom's party while her topaz gaze searched the vast hall.

The moment it touched him, genuine pleasure touched her bow-like mouth. It knocked him like a cool breeze on a hot day, fracturing something inside him wide open. He had hardly processed his own reaction, caught the answering jolt in his chest, when his cousin appeared at his table.

"Hello, Zayn."

Zayn covered his shock at his cousin's sudden appearance. He had known he was back in Sintar but he had been avoiding Zayn. Karim had always been snakelike, elusive and sneaky, which was why he was here today of all days.

Showing his face to Zayn here when he was busy with Mirah's wedding and the guests almost guaranteed that Karim could sneak away without causing himself any problems. One look at his cousin's fake smile reminded Zayn why he had never quite liked the man, even though they were of a similar age.

Suddenly now, it seemed Karim enjoyed everything— all the perks and pleasures of belonging to the royal family without any of the responsibilities and duties. An understanding that he had never resented before and yet was never far from Zayn's mind these days…

"You arrived in Sintar ten days ago. Why take this long to show yourself?"

"I didn't realize it was the sheikh's summons," Karim whined in that nasally voice.

Zayn gritted his jaw. How had he not known Amalia was right? Of course Karim had let someone else take the fall. "You were told it was official business."

"If it is to prod me toward some state job again, I will tell you the same as I told my mother, Zayn. I'm busy with my charities and business. I do not need a job at some junior level in your administration. Neither do I—"

When his words drifted off into ether, Zayn turned to his cousin.

Karim became pale beneath his untanned skin. "What is that woman doing here?"

Zayn followed his gaze to Amalia. Who turned in their direction just then. The last fragment of doubt he'd held on to even after evidence had been found, shattered at the pale cast of his cousin's face.

"Which hole have you been hiding in, Karim? That woman is my fiancée."

The entire vista of Amalia's face changed instantly. Her smile vanished and that same combative look that she had used on him those first few days entered her eyes. Alarm and amusement vied within Zayn, rendering him incapable of action for a few minutes.

She was loyal, passionate and generous, and he no longer wondered why Massimiliano had come after her or why he'd been so protective. Even with her independence and self-sufficiency, Amalia would always have that kind of effect on a man.

He sighed as she marched through the crowd toward them, a definitive set to her shoulders.

"That woman is stubborn, argumentative and a hound dog. You must be thinking with your—"

Zayn let Karim see the full force of his fury. Pounding his fists into his cousin at Mirah's wedding, he reminded himself, was a bad idea on many levels. "Careful, Karim. She is a woman I respect and admire. Do not force me to clean up your act with my own hands."

Karim stayed mute, a sulky light in his eyes.

"Now, you have two minutes before Amalia is here and raises the valid question of why I am not having you arrested right here, right now."

His face was chalk-white. "Arrested for what?"

"For possession of drugs, which you conveniently passed off on her brother."

"That's not true. I didn't even know her brother was—"

"I found the third man, Karim. He confessed to knowing that Aslam had nothing of that sort in his backpack. That leaves you. If you confess now, you can at least stop this from becoming a ruckus right now in front of the whole family. Even—"

"You can control your woman and stop it."

"No, I can't," Zayn said, another small fissure opening up in his chest. He could not control Amalia, neither could he control this irrational, inconveniently growing attachment of his to her, it seemed.

There were too many voices crowding in his head and the fact that he wanted to smash them all into silence told him he had become far too invested in his own facade and very little in the end.

The harshness in his voice when he spoke again was self-directed as much as it was on this weak man who had brought her into Zayn's life. "Though you deserve no such concession, I cannot shame my aunt in front of others. So leave now, and I better learn from the case detective by tonight that you have confessed your role in this."

Whatever spurious righteousness Karim had drummed up for this meeting disappeared when he noted the set tilt of Zayn's mouth. With no word, Karim left in the same sneaky way.

Leaning back into his chair, Zayn studied the woman rushing toward him like a sandstorm. Nothing had stayed the same since she'd marched into his life that day. Even now he felt as though he was standing on shifting sands, everything he had known in his life so far shaking in front of his eyes.

But he was Sheikh Zayn Al-Ghamdi and he had to do what was right for Khaleej, what was his duty.

Not what felt right in his gut.

His childhood friend, a fellow architect he had admired when he had been at college, a woman with revolutionary theories in medicine he had befriended, people who could have been friends and confidants, Zayn had bid goodbye because they were not suitable company for the Sheikh of Khaleej. But in months, if not days, they had become mere memories and he had moved forward with his life.

In mere weeks, Amalia would make her exit, too.

He would move forward again and she would become one of those memories.

"You let him go." Amalia forced the words past the disappointment turning her throat raw.

She rubbed the sleeve of her dress between her fingers, her entire body restless. It felt as if she was constantly trying to slow down time with her mind and each tick of every second, every sunrise, was pulling at her, trying to break her apart.

Only one more night before Mirah was married. As if that wasn't hard enough to come to terms with. Seeing the man who was responsible for her brother's plight calmly leave the hall twisted the knot in her stomach.

A cold smile in his eyes, Zayn looked distinctly unruffled. "Good morning to you, Amalia. Is it true that you took one of Mirah's fiancé's cousins by the collar yesterday afternoon?"

"Yes."

"Why?"

"He…was mouthing off."

"About you?"

"Does it matter?"

"Yes, because I had to smooth it over with his parents and apologize on your behalf for the emotional trauma you caused the boy."

"That's…you're impossible, Zayn. You immediately assumed I was guilty. I got a little physical with him because he was saying nasty things about you and when I called him on it, he started mouthing off about our relationship. The kid was a bully in the making and really, have you seen how big he is?"

"Apparently, now the parents think he will never get over his shock that women, especially tall, beautiful, angelic-looking women, could be so…offensive."

"You're laughing at me."

"I'm amused that you think I needed your defense."

"At that time I forgot what an arrogant ass you are," she said just to say something.

Because, like every morning and every evening and pretty much every time he looked at her, Amalia's breath ballooned in her chest at how gorgeous he was.

His pristine white shirt contrasted with the burnished bronze of his skin, emphasizing the virile masculinity of the man. Flutters emanated in the depth of her lower belly. Amalia shifted her gaze from his face to his throat. The strong column of it, her fingers longed to shape it like she had done last night. To feel the muscles in his shoulders clench under her fingertips, to feel the taut pressure when he moved inside her...

Flushed with unbidden heat, she moved to the table. His long, clever fingers drummed on the table, the same fingers that had been deep inside her heat...that drove her to maddening ecstasy every night...

"As flattered as I am by that look in your eyes, you're making me very uncomfortable in a public area, in the midst of everyone, and it will be at least afternoon before I can give you what you want, *habibti*."

A furious flush claimed her, and she looked away from him. "I don't know what you're talking about. I came to talk to you about that sneaky man and Aslam, not to—"

"It's nothing to feel defensive or shamed about, *latifa*. Believe me, I know exactly how you feel."

She lifted her gaze to him, her gut folding in on itself in anticipation. "You never...you don't..."

"Do I have to speak about how crazy you drive me with need for you to know, Amalia? We have spent every night together in the last month. Every night I tell myself that one more night will end the madness between us, that one more night of taking you, of feeling you writhe under me, will be enough...but it never works."

Dark hunger made the rugged landscape of his face even more breathtaking. "You know, it is only when this fire flares between us do you let me see all of you."

"I could say the same about you," Amalia whispered, longing coursing through her very blood. She looked around her to focus on something else, anything other than the words that fought to rise to her mouth, words that would push him away from her before she was ready to let go.

It didn't help the entirety of the guests being served in the vast hall had all focused on them. If not for Aslam, if not for Mirah, Amalia would have long happily… Aslam! Damn it, how could she forget why she couldn't wait to speak to Zayn?

Her gut felt like a hard knot. "Your cousin…how could you let that man leave?"

"I let him leave only from here."

"It took all these weeks to locate him and you just—"

"I told you I will take care of it."

"And Aslam continues to be in—"

"Amalia, sit down and calm yourself. You're drawing far too much attention."

"Because I am not shutting up about you, the Sheikh of Khaleej, letting a criminal slip out because he's your family."

His lips pulled back, a hardness entering his eyes. "No, you're drawing attention because you're raising your voice at your fiancé, who is currently surrounded by his guests, some of whom are state dignitaries and a wedding party, and all of whom would like nothing better than to point out that you lack the finesse and sophistication to deal with this in a sensitive and adult manner."

Amalia swallowed her gasp, his words pinching like sharp needles. It was one thing to hear from Mirah that Zayn's family, his advisers and the entire world did not think her suitable for the sheikh, quite different when he put it that way.

Dear God, she hadn't been hoping that something would change in the last few weeks, had she?

She felt like that little girl, confused and yet somehow aware of the painful reality of life. It felt like her heart was punctured inside her chest.

But she had come too far to give up now. "I don't care what they think about me."

"I do. Care about what they will say about you."

"You do?"

"Yes. Your reputation directly affects me."

Amalia had never felt this desperate struggle inside to be something she was not. Had never dreamt that falling in love would mean finding herself so inadequate to the man she loved. Being with Zayn was cleaving her within. "God forbid the sheikh is perceived as a weak man, a man who did not control his wayward fiancée, as a man who actually paid attention to anything coming out of a woman's mouth."

His eyes darkened into hard chips, his mouth a forbidding line. "Amalia, do not turn an age-old prejudice that has nothing to do with us into our fight. Do not turn your parents' disagreement into ours. I have never treated you with anything less than the respect you deserve. You forget that I'm not your lover, Zayn, all the time. I'm the sheikh and yes, I cannot be seen as not being able to stop my unruly fiancée from turning my sister's wedding breakfast into a ruckus about the justice system of Khaleej.

"Especially men and women I've been trying to appease with this whole charade."

He was not just angry, Amalia realized, her temper slowly losing its edge. It was more than his usually amused, tolerant annoyance at one of her blunt opinions. This was different.

This felt like withdrawal. Like he was retreating behind that damned mantle of his position. Like he was using her lack of discretion this moment to remind himself how unsuitable she was for him.

She wanted to scream; she wanted to walk away and hide in the privacy of her bedroom. But she did neither.

She settled down into the chair he had pulled out for her, a morass of emotions churning through her.

Her stomach slipped to her feet at all the curious faces that were watching her and Zayn. His parents' disapproval was like a force field even across the hall. No, she wouldn't feel as if she'd done something wrong just because she had lost her temper a little.

Then she saw Mirah and Farid at the main table and the fear mixed in with shock in Mirah's face. Shame filled her then. Mirah had been nothing but affectionate and welcoming to Amalia, even as she had realized that Amalia created waves among her family, even as she learned that some of Farid's family members disapproved of her.

Whether she had a right to be angry or not was moot. This was Mirah's day, a day she'd been looking forward to for quite a while.

She forced a smile to her lips and pulled her chair closer to Zayn's. With trembling fingers, she pushed at some imaginary speck on his collar. Filled the nerve-racking silence by telling him the morning she had had with a staff member and her stylist.

If it killed her, she'd not make a spectacle of herself. And him.

"Are you planning to kill me with that uncharacteristic inane chatter?" Zayn interrupted her in a dry voice that scratched against her senses. His thumb drew circles over her wrist, spreading a soft languor through her skin to every inch of her.

"Isn't that what you wanted?" she asked with fake sweetness.

"For you to act like there's nothing but cotton wool between your ears?" He sounded distinctly put out. "For you to simper at me with that fake smile and no real warmth in your eyes, no."

She sighed. "Sometimes I don't know what you want from me. Except—"

"Except?"

"Except when we're making...when we're having sex."

Something hard glittered in his eyes. Whatever anger she'd seen in his eyes until now, it was nothing like this fiery blaze that set his gaze alight. "You were going to say making love. You changed it to sex. Has your attitude toward that intimacy changed so much? Has it become so casual, then?"

"No, of course not," she protested hotly. She sighed and hid her face in his arm. How could she be angry with him when she'd provoked him on purpose? When it was this answer that she wanted from him?

When she probed him for answers while she couldn't tell him how she felt? Her time with him was counting down, mere days now, yet all she wanted was to forget Aslam, or Mirah or their respective positions in life and just be Amalia and Zayn.

The last thing she wanted to be was clingy when it was time to leave, but she wasn't able to harden her heart, either.

"I've never been this confused in my life," she said into the stretching silence. It was not the complete truth, but it was not a lie. "All I did in the last three weeks was accompany you to all the social events you bid me to, and look at some interesting issues when people courted my interest.

"And yet I'm called opinionated and too forward-thinking. All I was doing was just being—"

"You were just being yourself," Zayn finished for her, taking her hand in his on top of the table. "That is not your fault, Amalia. You're right, you did everything that I asked you to do."

But she was never going to be the right woman for

him. In a million years, she could not change herself and become the sort of woman everyone would approve of. Was this how her mother had felt with her father? Had there been no easy way to love her father without changing who she was?

She nodded, feeling a strange gush of tears at the back of her eyes. "How can I not be furious when you let him go?"

"Do you trust me, Amalia?"

Every logical thought said she shouldn't. It had been eight weeks since she'd walked into his study and except for allowing her to visit Aslam once and now letting the real culprit go, Zayn had done nothing to help her cause.

But every instinct, every irrational impulse that had absorbed everything about the man, screamed yes. "Yes, I do," Amalia finally whispered. "I think I trusted you from the beginning, Zayn, even when you were black-mailing me."

He laughed then, a hard, but genuine sound, and Amalia gazed up at him. Once again, they drew the attention of the crowd. But this time she knew it was because they were as mesmerized at the sight of him laughing as she was.

"I owe you an apology for not trusting your word. And that you had to resort to blackmail for what was right."

His apology, the tenderness in his eyes, sparked a joy inside her. "I liked blackmailing you, Sheikh."

Wicked amusement lit his gaze. "If my calculation of my cousin's character is right, he will confess in the next day. After that it will be a matter of days before Aslam is released. Just a matter of hours before you can see him."

Amalia shivered and instantly he held her close. "I can't wait to see him, to hug him."

"He is lucky to have you for his champion. I hope he learns to not throw away his life like this again. There's so much he could do."

The wistful note in his voice shook Amalia from within, that glimpse of the dreamer within. "And your cousin? Will he go to jail?"

"I do not know."

"But we both know that he is culpable. You told me yourself that your policy is harsh against drug offenders."

"Yes, but it is not in my hands to see his punishment matches his crime. My father or someone high up will interfere, because they will fear the reputation of the royal family, and his sentence will be lesser for that fact."

"How can you be so calm about that?"

"Nothing can be achieved by raging against things that you cannot change, Amalia. It is a lesson I learned very early in life."

"So much for making me believe that you're all powerful," she snorted, even as she understood what he meant.

If she had learned anything in the last two months, it was how delicately Zayn had to balance his actions with how the populace perceived him.

He couldn't be too forward, too westernized in his thoughts, nor could he let Khaleej live in the past. Progress and tradition had to be carefully weighed in every step he took in the name of the state. She wished she didn't; she wished she could see him as a ruthless statesman, as a playboy and not as a man sometimes caught between past and future, between his own dreams and his country's needs.

Because the more she saw that, the more Amalia felt as if she belonged by his side. Instead of wanting to run away from the challenges she would face, she felt energized by them; she felt as if this was what she was supposed to do.

To love this honorable man and be his mate in everything. To embrace her culture and her roots finally because Zayn embodied the best parts of it.

Except he was like an island, believing that his duty had to be carried out without an ounce of happiness in his own life.

Didn't he need someone who would walk that delicate balance with him, someone with whom he need not be the all-powerful sheikh and just Zayn, a man with vulnerabilities?

But she lacked the defiant courage to say that to him, to put her own deep feelings into words. She'd shared the most intimate moments of her life with him, but to open her heart to him, fear and pain at the prospect of his rejection rippled through her.

A wicked smile curved his mouth. "Now you know my darkest secret, *habibti*. Maybe I should make you a life-long prisoner so that you do not tell the world what Sheikh Zayn Al-Ghamdi is beneath what they see."

Amalia had never been so glad for being interrupted by Mirah at that minute. If Zayn had looked into her eyes, he would've known how much she wanted to be part of his life, even when it was an upward battle for her pretty much on every front.

CHAPTER ELEVEN

"Where are you going?"

Only after the question reverberated in the bedroom did Zayn realize how accusatory and childish he sounded. No, not just sounded. That was how he felt.

As if he was being pulled in polarizing directions, being split in between. As though he was being told again and again by a relentless voice that his life was different, that his life was not ordinary.

"Love is a weakness for other people, a fantasy, an indulgence we cannot afford, Zayn."

His father's derisive words were like little worms inside his head, and he took a deep breath trying to banish the turmoil he felt inside.

It was impossible that this turmoil, this constant confusion, could be love. He didn't even know what love was, truly. He didn't know how deep and abiding a connection could be between a man and a woman.

All he knew was he still hadn't quite driven out the attraction, the lust he felt for Amalia. Given that she was the first woman who had integrated into aspects of his life that had never even known a woman, it followed that he felt a connection with her.

A connection he was not prepared to sever just yet.

"I asked you something, Amalia."

Her hands stilled on the bag she was packing, but she didn't turn around instantly. He hated when she did that, when she hid her reaction from him, when she pulled some facade together so that he couldn't even guess what was going on in her mind.

In five days of the most lavish celebrations and ceremonies around Mirah's wedding, all he had seen was what the rest of the world saw.

Amalia Noor Hadid Christensen, as the Khaleej media had taken to calling her once her roots and her background had been discovered. Poised, stylish, the perfect ornament on the sheikh's arm, with a ready smile for the guests or the media. As Mirah's wedding day neared, it was as if the light had gone out from her eyes. She had retreated so far behind her mask that even Zayn began to long for her impertinent remarks and her blunt honesty.

The rip of the zipper on her bag hurtled him out of his brooding thoughts.

She finally turned around, her gaze implacable. "Mirah is having a kind of girls' night with her friends in her wing tonight. As she is leaving with her husband tomorrow." She darted from her bedroom to the open area near the pool and he prowled after her. The charge that was never far behind between them built up, even more electrifying for she was leading him on a chase.

Something savage and atavistic filled Zayn for they both knew how this was going to end, how tonight was going to play out. His pulse raced, his muscles tightening already.

"She invited me over and I thought I would make a night out of it."

"Do you have to pack all your things for one night?" he asked again, walking around the pool, following her, just as she picked up a paperback from one of the alcoves.

He closed his mind and instantly, the image of her spread out on the low divan with a book in her hand flashed. Always, he realized that image would haunt him now.

With a frown, he looked around the house he had poured all his dreams into. Every nook and cranny was now touched with memories of Amalia.

He reached her at the entrance of his own bedroom and blocked her exit. A nightgown and her iPad were in her hands this time. He had hid the iPad two nights ago when she wouldn't give him the attention he wanted.

She had squealed and tried to get away, and he had tackled her until they had both fallen to the rug in a heap. And then he had covered her body with his, desperate to possess her. The same insistent desire filled him now, blinding him to everything else.

The freedom he found with her, the ecstasy when he sank deep into her…it was a drug he would forever crave.

"I thought it a good idea to pick up my stuff. Six weeks is a long time and I have strewn small things around everywhere."

When she turned to step out, he blocked the entrance. Skin flushed, mouth trembling, she would not even meet his gaze. "Zayn—"

One arm stretched out to stop her, he leaned against the other side. "I did not think I would see the day when you would be so intimidated by me that you would not even meet my gaze, Amalia."

Shoulders went back; she glared at him. "I hope that day never comes."

His hands found her shoulders, automatically tipping her body toward his. "You've been avoiding me for the past few days. Actually, since that morning breakfast."

She didn't shy her gaze this time, but conveniently hid it in his chest. His heart rumbled against her cheek, a reaction he was used to now. "There were a lot of places I needed to be. Mirah was counting on me."

"And today?" he asked. When she would have danced away from him, he snaked both arms around her. Shaping the curve of her bottom, he pulled her flush against him. He couldn't stop touching her, couldn't stop the passion from flaring between them at a moment's notice. "Would you rather spend it with Mirah or her brother?"

Amalia knew she should say Mirah or a hundred other destinations that didn't have the man. But she was weak, irrevocably in love with him, hungry for every second she could spend with him. In his arms. Her flesh was trembling and weak after avoiding him for four days.

A gloriously savage smile curving his lips, he kissed her possessively, instantly filling her with wanton heat. One touch of those gorgeous lips was enough to ready her for his possession, enough to make her cling to him with a keening groan.

She clung to him and pressed her lips to his neck when he lifted her into his arms and carried her to the pool area. A soft gasp left her as the raw beauty of the house overwhelmed her again.

A sky dotted with silver jewel-like stars reflected in the pool below, making the surface of water ripple and glitter like a jewel itself. Moroccan lanterns around the pool provided just enough light for them to see their way. The smell of rose incense drifted from somewhere, filling the air with the voluptuous tendrils of it.

She had never imagined herself in a place such as this, true. But it was the man who had her breath fluttering in and out of her throat, her limbs liquid and aching.

Barely out of breath, he carried them to an alcove that gave the best view of the sky and the pool.

When he slid her to her feet and reached for the zipper of her dress, Amalia stayed his hand. "The staff…"

"Did you not realize that no one is allowed here, especially during the night, *habibti*?" His low whisper strummed at her nerves. Fingers danced over the skin he bared, pressing and stroking. "I did not want anyone to hear the sounds you make when you come. I could not take the chance that one of them could walk by and see your silky skin, or those pouty breasts, or the way you drape those legs around me when you sleep.

"You are mine, Amalia. Something savage awakens in me when I think of any other man even looking at your beautiful body or hearing those little whimpers you make."

Her mouth dry, Amalia stood awash in the sensations that pummeled her.

She was his. She wanted to be his in every waking moment, not just in the dark intimacy of the night.

But before she could even form the words, he rid her of her fitted sheath dress and her strapless bra, leaving her in her bikini panties. The cold breeze kissed her nudity and she shivered. Only when his own skin, heated and like rough velvet touched her, did Amalia realize that he had already shed his clothes, too.

Slowly, pockets of heat began to emerge on her cold skin, until in mere seconds, she was burning with need.

Turning her around so that she could see their outlines in the pool, he pressed his mouth into her shoulder. Rough bristles scraped against the sensitive skin. Amalia would have melted to the tiles on the floor if he wasn't holding her up.

"From the minute you walked in here that day and looked around you with such wonder, I have dreamed of taking you like this. Out in the open, with the sky and the stars witness to this magic between us…"

By the time he was rolling her nipples with his fingers, Amalia was already panting. Her flesh damp and ready for him. Melting her skin with his kisses, he brought them to the ground.

Smiling when she protested, he pulled her over on top of him, until she was straddling him. Different sensations, an even more stringent awareness, drenched Amalia.

She closed her eyes when he moved his palm from the valley between her breasts to her abdomen that clenched with need and then finally to her core. A groan ripped from her when he tested her readiness.

"You astride me, with your glorious hair falling about you, and the jeweled sky in the background. It's all the Bedouin inside me wants. Take me inside you, *ya habibti*."

Greedy for him, Amalia reached for him and guided his hot, thick erection into her. He held her hips loosely, letting her set the pace. The first slide of his turgid flesh inside her channel sent her head back.

"Tell me how it feels," he demanded, his voice thick and hoarse.

Amalia couldn't bear to move yet. Nor open her eyes and look at him. "The pleasure is intense. Zayn, you...you feel like you're everywhere inside me."

His hands slowly moved to her buttocks then and taking the cue, Amalia wiggled. Their groans ripped the silent air, the sound drifting into the sky.

She slapped her palms on his chest, tilted her body forward until he almost pulled out of her.

The tight, bruising clasp of his fingers over her, the veins stretching in his neck, told her how much he was rearing to take control. That it stretched the edges of his desire to give her the lead.

Reveling in the sheer power of rendering such a man

out of his control, Amalia straightened and moved up and down again.

Hard and filthy, his words sent a thrill through her. With every thrust, she learned what this fiercely gorgeous man wanted, learned what increased her own pleasure.

And then she set a rhythm that set all the wildness of her love that she hid free. Here, there was no distance between them. Here, she didn't fear rejection.

In that moment they were perfect for each other. Only with each other were they complete.

Sweat coated her skin. Amalia clenched her inner muscles tighter just as Zayn stroked her clit.

Throwing her head back, she cried out, tears pouring down her cheeks at the intensity of the pleasure. His hard upward thrusts filled her body, riding the wave of her orgasm. The hard slap of his thrusts chased the contractions in her muscles, making her limbs molten. His hard body jerked under her as he came with an explosive growl.

She fell on top of him, feeling as if she had broken apart into a thousand pieces.

Her panting breaths fell on his damp skin as he held her tight against him. Every time he was inside her, every time they shared this explosive fire, her defenses were shattered, too.

She closed her eyes and willed herself to remember every texture of his skin, the scent of his damp body, the clench of his muscles, the beauty of this hard man who possessed a big heart.

For it was time for her to leave.

"Zayn, we have to talk."

"No, we don't. I don't care if Mirah invited your favorite rock star, Amalia. You're not leaving my side tonight."

"I'm not talking about tonight. I want to discuss something important."

His hand slid blatantly between her thighs and already, a wanton thrill began again at her sex. She became shamelessly damp again, a groan rising out of her against her own will. Ready for him again.

If he moved that thumb that was languorously resting against the swollen bud at her sex, if he even touched those lips to her skin, Amalia knew she would not recover tonight. And another night and another night would pass on while the long days would gouge her with hope and hollow her with wanting.

Waiting to be told that their charade was over.

Waiting to be told that Zayn Al-Ghamdi did not need her anymore.

Waiting to feel her heart ripped out of her chest...

She needed to leave while she still had a little of herself intact, before he completely crushed her.

"I want to talk about us, our relationship. This can't wait till morning."

He released her so fast, all the desire disappeared from his face so quickly that Amalia would have laughed if she wasn't so close to crying again. Feeling as though more than just her body was nakedly vulnerable to him, she pulled the blanket he had covered them with earlier around her.

He obviously felt no such self-consciousness. Still, she had to have this conversation and Amalia needed it to be without an evidence of what she was walking away from. So she stood up along with her blanket, reached for another one and threw it at him.

His mouth twitched but thankfully, he said nothing about her continual shyness with him. Not that he hadn't awakened her into all kinds of wanton desires...

"Is this a discussion we have to have tonight?"

Dragging a forceful breath into her lungs, she held on to the anger that rose through her. "You need not look so alarmed. I just...I wanted to talk about our plans."

"I'm not alarmed. I am..." He clutched his nape with his hand, and the muscles in his chest shifted, tempting her. "This is the first night we have had some privacy, a little time with each other in over a week." He sounded like a little boy and Amalia stared at him in consternation.

"Zayn..."

But the moment of vulnerability was already gone. "Tell me, what is it?"

"I...need to make plans. Mirah is happily married to a man who will love her for the rest of her life, thanks to you."

"And you," he added, his mouth flattening.

She shrugged. "I heard from one of your aides today that Aslam will be released any day now. Once I make sure he is okay, I need to leave—"

"Back to Massi and your waiting life?"

"You know how I feel about him and yet you continually—"

He pulled her to him suddenly, a blaze of emotion in his eyes. "Because I'm jealous of your friendship with him. This is what you do to me, Amalia."

Her breath slammed hard into her throat. "This is about us. Now that we've accomplished both our goals, I need to go back to my life. I can't put it on hold forever. Neither for Aslam nor for you. At some point, I have to walk out of this fantasy and back into reality."

"You do not have to leave Sintar yet." *Or me.* His unsaid words fluttered in the air.

Hope fluttered in her chest like a fragile bird's tiny wings. "What...what do you mean?"

"You were right. Mirah is married and as much as a poll comes out every week about your unsuitability to be the next sheikha, Khaleej and its populace, my family, my staff, the entire world, believes we are together. That you've thoroughly enchanted me. Apparently, you are the modern-day Cinderella.

"Why ruin it when we don't have to?"

"You want me to stay in Sintar?"

"Yes. With me, here at the palace."

If her heart beat any faster, Amalia was afraid it would burst right out of her chest. "Zayn, I don't know what to—"

"Thanks to your blackmailing scheme, I do not have to worry about marriage for a little while. And I do not see why we cannot continue to enjoy each other, continue this pretense until I have to do the duty thing again."

Pain was an arrow in her chest, a knife lodged in her ribs. Words wouldn't rise to her lips past her raw throat. "You still intend to look for some suitable candidate?"

"Yes. I can indulge myself for a short while, Amalia, but in the end, I will need a sheikha…"

Amalia rose to her feet so swiftly that her head whirled for a second. She had been right. He would never see her as anything but unsuitable. Never give her a chance.

She raised her chin, draping her pride and self-respect like a blanket over her breaking heart. "As good as it is to know that you have it all worked out according to your plans and life, I'm afraid that will not work for me, Zayn."

Something hard entered his eyes at the way she had imitated his formal speech. "And why is that?"

"You see, just like you, I have some expectations for myself, if not a kingdom's. And since I joined this whole living away from the shadow of past a little too late, I intend to make up for lost time.

"A toxic relationship that's predestined to go nowhere

while I fall more and more into its depths…" Her voice wobbled here, her grief over losing him overpowering her stupid pride. "That reminds me far too much of a fate my mother lived.

"If there's one thing I have learned in these six weeks, in our torrid affair, it is that I don't have to live my life based on anyone's fears or hang-ups. And that includes you and this notion you have, this template you have of what kind of woman would suit you."

He clutched her arms, his grip painful. Tears filling her eyes, Amalia struggled to not sink into his embrace. "You have always known where this was going."

"Yes, I did. And I'm saying enough now. Before you completely break me. Before you make me into a shadow who could never recover her old self.

"Don't do that to me, Zayn. Don't make me regret knowing you. Please don't make me hate you and myself."

Such a fierce glow burned in his eyes. Amalia shivered violently, seeing the knowledge that dawned in his eyes. They both knew how powerless she was to resist him again and again… They both knew that in that minute, all he had to do was to cover the distance between their seeking mouths and she would agree to stay…

But slowly his grip on her loosened. And he walked away without a word.

Amalia crumpled to her knees on the tiles, disappointment and relief and every other emotion crushing her.

CHAPTER TWELVE

HANDS TUCKED INTO the pockets of his trousers, Zayn stood at the window of his study, looking out over the grounds that surrounded the palace. The last few weeks had been the hardest of his life. He had buried himself in work, driving himself at a relentless pace that had strained his staff to the maximum as if he could run far and fast from the desolation that seemed to be weighing him down if he took a moment to breathe.

Duty over personal happiness…it had been a tenet by which he'd lived all his life and yet, that same duty lost its satisfaction for him. The more he worked for the betterment of Khaleej, the more resentful of it he grew.

For it was a steep price he had to pay.

Amalia had shattered the cold aloofness he had built into a shell around him, reaching a part of him that he had buried deep.

He had spent all morning on his phone and still, he had no idea where she was. Morning had given way to noon, sunlight glittering over the gardens in the courtyard.

Had he drifted here because this was where he had met her first? Had she so thoroughly written him off that she had made herself so unreachable? Only one man could have helped her, and the idea of Amalia with Massi burned an acrid hole in his gut.

Regrets piled over him. He should have never let her leave him in the first place. He shouldn't have taken so long to break out of his own shell, to realize that his world was empty without her by his side, that he couldn't even stomach the idea of some faceless, docile woman… The thought that she might be permanently lost to him carved paths through him, making him utterly restless.

He had never felt so alone; never had the burden of Khaleej felt so unbearable. He didn't even want to face his father.

He had never been a gambling man and yet, he had taken this chance. Had hoped that the thought of his wedding would somehow bring Amalia back to him.

The creak of the door made him turn, his heart jumping into his chest.

He let out a harsh breath when he saw that his guest was Benjamin Carter. Newly wed and nauseatingly in love, the New York tycoon was the last man Zayn wanted to see.

At least with the rest of the palace and its staff, no one dared to point out the obvious with him. That he was to be married in hours and his bride was missing.

"It has come to my attention that you're missing a bride, Sheikh," the American drawled, a lazy twitch to his mouth. "Is it possible that our esteemed Ms. Young was unable to convince a woman to take you on?"

Zayn rolled his eyes. "Since you're my invited guest and your bride will clearly be horrified by the result, I will refrain from messing up your face, Carter. Now leave me in peace."

Any other man would have cowered at the steel in his tone. However, as he had expected, the warning barely registered on the man. His gaze, at least, lost that wicked smile. "Your staff is in uproar, your PR people don't know if they should issue a statement. This could easily become another big scandal, Sheikh. Even if your sister is happily married, your reputation could still—"

"In your slang, Carter, I don't give a damn."

"Where is the woman you're supposed to marry?"

Despite the void in his gut, Zayn found it easy to answer. Maybe because Carter was one of those few people in the world who wasn't intimidated by the mantle of power that Zayn carried. "Not supposed to, Carter. The woman I want to marry."

Carter's gaze cleared, as if the meaning was clear. "Yeah? So where is she?"

The expression on the other man's face made Zayn crack a smile. "I don't know where she is. I don't know if she will show up, either."

"But she knows that she's marrying you today, yes?" Now he sounded as if Zayn had lost his mind.

Maybe he had. Maybe waiting for a woman he hadn't even asked to marry him was foolish. But if this talk of his wedding didn't ferret Amalia out, nothing would. He would have a mess to clean up come tomorrow, but Zayn found he didn't give a damn right now.

Zayn shook his head and a filthy curse fell from Carter's mouth.

"This is not some strange custom in Khaleej, is it, Sheikh? That the groom doesn't know if the bride's going to show up?"

"I should feel insulted, I think, but I know you mean well, Carter. And no, it is no strange custom."

He had defied all customs and traditions by falling in love. He didn't think Amalia was unsuitable for him anymore. It was he that fell short of the kind of man Amalia deserved.

He had incredible power at his hands; he was probably one of the wealthiest men in the world, but he would not be able to give her unlimited time if she spent her life with him. Nor could he give her a loving, welcoming family.

Except for Mirah, he had no doubt that most of his family would give her the cold treatment. For most of her life, she would be made to feel like an outsider.

She would have to trade so many things that she could have with any other man to be with him. If he had any sense, he would just let her go.

But Zayn realized he was also selfish when it came to her. Giving up architecture, unsuitable friends, personal happiness, they were nothing when he thought of how empty his life would be without Amalia by his side.

"Then I need a drink and it's clear that you need one, too, Sheikh. So why don't you—?"

The door slammed open again and this time, Amalia stood at the threshold. Mouth trembling, chest rising and falling, she looked blazingly furious. "*You*...arrogant, heartless, cold brute. How could you?"

His heart thudded against his chest. Something twisted and settled deep in him, an overwhelming urge to take her in his arms and hide her away in the desert. Where she would never have another opportunity to escape him.

He smiled at that imagery—that would be as palatable to Amalia as him dragging her by her hair into his cave... Throat tight and air gushing from his lungs, he couldn't quite hold himself together.

His bluff had worked. But it was still a long way to go. Pride came to his rescue. "I believe heartless and cold mean the same thing, Amalia." It was the only way left to him to fight the lost feeling that had surrounded him for three weeks.

He was not good with this feeling of inadequacy, this self-doubt. He did not like that he was going to have to finesse the deal of his lifetime and he had less to offer than the other party.

Twin spots sat high on her cheeks as she curled her mouth in that threatening way of hers. "You don't want to mess with me today, Zayn. Maybe you've forgotten, but I'm very good at blackmailing, remember? And the whole world, once again, would love to hear what I have to say about His Royal Highness Sheikh Zayn Al-Ghamdi."

Shock made Zayn silent while Carter's laughter boomed in the room like the explosions of firecrackers.

She cast a glance at Benjamin, her chest falling and rising. "Can I have a few minutes with the sheikh?"

That lazy smile returning to his mouth, Carter nodded. To Zayn, he said, "I assume the wedding is on, Sheikh? Should I alert your staff to the fact?"

If there was a moment when Zayn would have happily forgotten that they were supposed to be adult men and not pummel each other, it was this. He kept his eyes on Amalia, saw the anger in hers and caught the urge. "Yes," he said irritably. He hated the weak feeling in his gut, this feeling of being out of control. Nothing in his life had prepared him for this.

"Ms. Christensen, I suppose," Carter asked and Amalia nodded. "Give him hell."

The door closed behind Carter, leaving them in a stark silence. For a few seconds all they did was stare at each other. He had faced so many daunting situations in his life—political and financial with innumerable lives in his hand, and yet, the tension that was strummed through every inch of him was a stranger.

"Amalia—"

"You said you were going to wait a few months. It's been barely a month since I left and this date… God, this was the date we told people *we* would be marrying. I just…"

She ran a trembling hand to push a lock of hair out of her eyes and that was when finally Zayn noticed it.

It felt like a punch to his gut, a slap of rejection.

She had cut her hair. Those long waves that he'd loved wrapping around his fingers, that had caressed his body with a silken touch, they caressed her face and jaw now, giving her an elfin-like look.

But since he meant to begin the way he wanted to go on, he pursed his mouth. He needed her in his life like no other but he didn't want their life to become one battle after another. There were going to be enough battles to fight together without their personal life becoming one, too.

"You cut your hair," he said, accusation high in his tone.

Her fingers drifted through her shoulder-length locks. Defiance made her eyes glimmer like precious jewels. "I wanted something different, something that didn't make me think of you every day."

Another punch, another roughly indrawn breath. "And it was as simple as cutting off your hair?" Something he had adored.

She shrugged. And when the furor in his chest calmed down, when he let instinct, the newly discovered emotions in his gut, drive him rather than plain facts and logic, Zayn remembered that she did that when she didn't want to quite tell the truth.

She was here, he reminded himself again. She had come blasting through his doors at the idea of his wedding. That was the start he had wanted.

"Where have you—"

"I didn't come here to answer your questions or to be harassed by you."

Why had he thought this was going to be easy? He had little enough experience dwelling on and talking about his feelings…only a handful of times when he had even felt such strong emotions…and this was Amalia, who turned everything into a battle. He sighed. "Why are you here, then?"

"I came to give you a piece of my mind."

"And where have you been for the last month?" The question slipped through his lips, bitter jealousy tugging at the reins of his control.

"With…" Again that infernal shrug. "That doesn't matter. I needed to come because—"

"Is Aslam in trouble again?"

"Will you stop interrupting me as if I'm one of your staff members? This is hard enough as it is," she mumbled at the end.

Only now did he realize the dark circles under her eyes, the pinched cut of her features. "I was merely curious about Aslam. I thought I would keep an eye on him for you but my staff could not even locate him."

She stared at him, as if she didn't know what to make of that. And her startled disbelief that he could care about even such a small thing as her brother's welfare made his ire rise. "Is that so hard to believe?"

"Yes. No…" Her lashes flicked down and she moved away from him. He saw her swallow forcefully before she did that. "He…is making changes in his life, the right ones. You were right. That time he spent in the jail, I think it made him see that he was heading toward utter ruin if he continued like that. He's thinking of returning to college."

"I am glad, for your sake more than his. I know how much you love him."

She shrugged, a sheen of wetness coating her eyes. The slight tremble of her mouth, the shuddering breath she drew, it hit Zayn like a blow to the chest.

"Yes, but love is not always enough, is it? I have found

out that my father loved my mother just as much as she loved him, but they could not make it work."

"You went to see him?"

She nodded, a lone tear carving a path on her cheek. "Aslam refused to let me leave. Nor would he go with me. He kept saying I belonged in Sintar with—"

"You do." His statement fell in between them like the pounding of a gavel.

"When he heard of Aslam's release, my father came to see us at the hotel…I realized I couldn't be a coward for the rest of my life. It was time to face him."

"You're the last woman on earth I would call cowardly, Amalia."

She blanched, her skin losing every ounce of color.

"Is it so hard to think that I think well of you, Amalia?"

"Whether you think I'm strong or beautiful or intelligent, it doesn't matter, does it, Zayn? Not when you think…"

Silence ensued between them again fraught with tension and their emotions, things that were rearing to break out into the open. Zayn felt as if he was going to break from the inside out.

Her shoulders shaking, Amalia looked like a slight breeze would fell her, too. Only then he realized how much it would have cost her to come here today, when she would have had to see the woman he would've chosen.

And in the face of that vulnerability, pride and self-respect and arrogance, everything dissolved. That she would take this step toward him when he'd done nothing but use her was humbling and even disconcerting. Love, it seemed, given and returned, was a roller coaster, one minute exaltation and the next, utter desperation.

"There is no bride here today."

She frowned. The tremor that went through her lithe

body was far too obvious to miss. "No bride…what does that mean?" She pushed her hair back from her face, a gesture left over even though she cut the thick waves. And it tugged at him as nothing could.

She looked toward the door, her body poised for flight and then turned toward him again. The frown deepened into a scowl. "But there are guests flying in from the neighboring countries and from your own family. There are network station crews everywhere waiting to telecast…how the hell can you not have a bride, Zayn?"

Zayn came to her and took her hands in his. Never had his heart beat so rapidly. "I forgot to ask the bride to marry me. So she doesn't know. I was just hoping against hope that she would show up. Carter thinks I've lost my mind and I believe he is right."

Comprehension dawned on her face and she jerked her hands away from him. "This was all…"

"Amalia—"

"You're a manipulative jerk!"

"Manipulative? You disappeared off the face of the earth. You would not take my calls, you cut me off from your life as thoroughly as you did your father."

"Because my heart was breaking and there was only so much of you I could resist before I weakened and stayed for as long as you wanted me."

"You do not know how much I regret putting you through that, how much I wish…" Tenderness filled his gaze, stealing what little rationality Amalia was trying to hold on to. "Will you marry me? Today?"

"Is this some kind of political face-saving?"

"No. In fact, I've had advisers continually offer infernal advice that you might not be a good candidate to be my sheikha."

"I heard enough of that while I was here. And I think

you and your damned advisers are all wrong. That's what I came to tell you."

"That's what you came to tell me…" he repeated, a little spark of hope fluttering to life inside him. Her wrist bones were delicate in his hands, almost fragile. And yet she held his happiness, his future, in her hands. "Tell me, then."

"I think your assumption that you can't have even a small flicker of happiness in your life is wrong. Your assumption that I would somehow detract you from your duty, somehow minimize your power, is even more absurd.

"I understand about duty and selflessness more than you think.

"I put my life on hold for so many years to look after my mom. And I never once weakened, or resented her for it. I would never weaken you, Zayn. How could I?

"There have been kings and presidents and heads of state all over the world throughout history who married for love, who chose to reach for a little personal happiness, too, and they have only thrived.

"If you think I would become a liability to you—" her voice caught here, her throat a mass of emotions "—then you're not the man I thought."

A gold blaze flared in his eyes, drenching her entire being in a joy that she couldn't contain. "And if I told you that I came to the same conclusion, only a little slower than you? That I could shoulder all the responsibility in the world if I have you by my side, that you make everything joyful, meaningful?"

There was no stopping her tears now. Her heart thundered into life as if all it had been doing until now was pump blood. "You tricked me! You still think this is some kind of power struggle between us. You…"

"You left me no choice but to trick you. I…could not

find you and I…went crazy imagining all kinds of scenarios."

"I was never in any kind of trouble, Zayn."

"Trouble? No." A stark need filled his eyes then. "You're the most capable woman I have ever known, Amalia. Some nights I found myself fervently wishing you weren't so strong and independent, so stubborn that—"

Throat raw, she said, "I know what you wish I was, but this is who I am."

"You misunderstand me. It took you—your strength, your spirit, your independence—all of you to unlock my heart. So much that I have this unbearable feeling inside my chest that it is I who is not enough for you. My worry was that you must have realized you deserved a man who recognized that, who loved you like you should be loved.

"I was terrified that you went back to Massi, had written me off completely."

Amalia could do nothing but stare at Zayn, at the vulnerability that punctured every word he uttered. She went to him then, any anger she'd held on to as a defense melting at the warmth in his words.

He clutched her to him hard, driving the breath out of her lungs. Hard body shuddered around her, telling her more than his words ever could. He loved her, she knew it now, even if he had yet to say it. But feelings and emotions were hard for him. He'd been trained to view them as weaknesses, trained to believe that he needed no one and nothing.

He had taken an enormous risk on her, this man who didn't put one step wrong if he thought it would hurt Khaleej and the perception about him. He had made himself vulnerable for her. And for now that had to be enough.

They all kept crowing she was far too opinionated, far too independent to be good for him, didn't they? Well, she was. And she couldn't bear for him to second-guess himself. "I've never loved and will never love a man like I love you, Zayn. What do I have to do to make you believe that?"

His fingers clasped her face, and such sheer happiness, such liquid joy, dawned in his eyes that Amalia forgot to breathe. Just that smile of his was enough to hurtle her into falling in love with him all over again. A smile, she knew, no one but she had witnessed. That was all for her, only her.

A jagged breath left him as he leaned his forehead against hers. "My heart belongs to you, *ya habibti*. This feeling, this cavernous void in my chest as if I had left an essential part of me somewhere, as if I would never feel whole again…I have never felt anything like it. I have never resented everything I have to be as I do when you're not with me.

"You've opened my heart. I love you, Amalia."

His mouth covered hers then and Amalia melted into his touch. Every cell, every inch of her, felt like it was touched with light, with a piercing sharp awareness. Lacing her fingers around his nape, she moved under his expert caresses hungrily, opening up for him, like a flower did for a sun. The fluid power of his lean body, the hard rattle of his heart against hers, she had never felt more powerful; never had she reveled so much in being alive.

A shiver danced over her spine as he widened his legs and cradled her, as his erection imprinted itself against her belly. A month of separation had only made the need to know him in that intimacy that much keener. It was fueled by fear, too, for only in bed, only when they were sharing that deepest intimacy, did Zayn open up to her.

She moved her hands to his lean hips, desperate to have him inside her again. Laughing against her mouth, he pulled back, after he drew her body into a punishingly raw response.

"I would love for nothing but to take you here, *latifa*, but…" He looked so drugged that Amalia laughed. "I remembered. Where were you, Amalia?"

"With Aslam and my father."

"I wish you had let me be there with you. I wish you had let me be your strength."

"But you made me see myself through new eyes. Made me question everything I had ever believed. I was so angry by what my father had done by sending me away with her, I clutched all my mother's complaints about him and let them feed my hatred.

"If I hated him, I would never have to face the hurt. When I left here, I was so angry with you and with him. With myself. That anger was good, positive."

"What did he say?"

"I'm still angry with him for giving up on me so easily but I understand why he did it. Mom was always prone to these periods of extreme joy, then would come volatile periods and then these deep, dark periods where nothing could jolt her out of it.

"And their differences and the pressures of marriage didn't help. When he suggested she needed to seek medical help, she flew off the handle. Even I remember that day when I blocked out everything else. He told me how he realized that life with him made everything only that much harder for her.

"It was the day she told him she wanted a divorce."

Zayn scowled. "I don't understand. He thought that she might be suffering from depression and he still let you go with her. That's the height of negligence."

She shrugged, and he knew she was still fighting the same fight. He held her in the circle of his arms, wishing he could somehow take away her pain. He wanted nothing in the world to hurt her and yet, a life with him would only be a challenge for her. But he was determined to make up for it, to love her that much more. He would never let her doubt how much he loved her, how important she was to him.

"You do not have to forgive him or give him a place in your life, *azeezi*. If it's easier for you to face it, hate him. We will never see him again."

Eyes shining with unshed tears, she looked up at him. "It hurts, but I see it, Zayn. She promised him she would seek help if he let her have one of us without contest, if he never came back into her life again.

"And he gave me to her instead of Aslam."

"Because you were the more stable one," Zayn gritted out. He looked so angry on her behalf that Amalia almost worried for her father. "He knew how much she was going to lean on you. He made you an adult long before you were one."

"He had no choice and he loved her far too much, I think. More than he loved me or Aslam. And once I left, he had his hands full with Aslam and then his new family. And although she kept her word to him and sought medical help, I think she never forgave him for giving up on her, for not fighting for her."

Hiding her face in his chest, she took a deep breath. "He…he was so upset when he learned what happened between us." Zayn stiffened around her and she hurried, "I didn't tell him about the blackmail part, just that I… fell in love with you.

"We stayed up the whole night talking. I think he was hoping that I'd walk away from you. He said he only saw problems ahead for us."

"I told him we were nothing like them but he said we have it that much harder."

"He is right, Amalia. I could not lie to you about what lies ahead for—"

It felt like the bottom fell away from under her feet. Again. "What are you saying?"

"That I love you so much that, apparently, I have to put your happiness above my own, *habibti*. A life with me will not be easy on you. A royal life is never without pressures but—"

"You think I'm not aware of it. I came fully prepared to take you on and anyone else who stood in my way, Zayn. I…I think if we love each other truly—"

"There is no *if* about it, *latifa*. I'm lost without you."

Her heart on wings, Amalia kissed him hard. "Then we should be able to conquer anything that comes our way. I know I want to be with you more than anything I have ever wanted in life."

"Will you be my wife, then, Amalia? My sheikha? Will you marry me tonight because I cannot part with you for one more night?"

Amalia nodded, and he took her mouth in a tender kiss that was a promise from the man, and surrender from the sheikh himself.

EPILOGUE

Five years later

THE STARS IN the moonlit sky shone in the dark water beneath, making it look as if they belonged on earth, in that pool, in the house where Amalia made a home with her husband, Sheikh Zayn Al-Ghamdi.

After a month tour of Europe by her husband's side, along with their son and daughter and their entourage, Amalia was glad to be home. It was hard to travel with their itinerary being so full, with kids and nannies and aides, but she wouldn't trade it for anything in this world.

She far preferred to have at least glimpses of her husband at a dinner with politicians rather than not see him for weeks on end. They argued ferociously at times, they compromised sweetly sometimes, but to be never apart more than necessary, to work out their differences and share their dreams... Amalia had never even imagined that she would love so deeply, so completely and have it in return.

It had taken five years of marriage for the media and the populace of Khaleej to finally understand that Amalia had every intention of being her husband's confidante and friend and ally and lover on top of his dutiful wife. That she went on diplomatic tours with her husband. Even when she had been pregnant with Rafiq and Lilah. That she wouldn't quietly sit in his shadow. That her husband and she shared a true marriage of hearts.

The unconventional sheikha, she'd been named. And she'd grown into it happily.

The conservatives, of course, went on a rabble every time she expressed her views but both she and Zayn had long understood that it was more out of habit and principle than any real objection to her.

With her cup of tea in hand, Amalia retreated to one of the cozy nooks. Propping her feet upon the low divan, she closed her eyes.

She loved this house as much as she loved the man who had designed it.

"I thought you would be in bed by now."

She put her cup aside and moved over as Zayn settled down next to her on the divan. "You're done for the night?"

With a chuckle, he nodded. "Is there much left of it?" He unbuttoned his shirt and pulled it out of his trousers. The power in his frame still made her breath catch. Even after five years. "I'm sorry, I know this is the first night we have had to ourselves since we returned but—"

Amalia covered his lips with her finger and pressed into him shamelessly. "You're here now."

"I missed you, *azeezi*."

His arm went around her, his large body coating hers with a warmth she could never get enough of. She turned into his touch eagerly and touched her mouth to his in a lazy kiss. His fingers crawled up her nape and into her hair, holding her still for him. Tendrils of want awoke within her, the raw possession of his touch making her desperate.

"It was nice of Aslam to take the kids," Zayn said in a voice laced with dark honey. Nimble fingers pushed away the straps of her nightdress, working their way to her breast. Her breath caught, a tight wave of pleasure claiming her lower belly.

"Zayn…" She groaned, stretching into his touch, like a cat. "I wanted to talk about the Center for Women's—"

The rest of her words morphed into a groan as her wicked husband pushed her into the divan and covered her with his hard body. Instantly, she wrapped her legs around his hips and cradled his thick erection. "Tonight I do not want the sheikha, nor the razor-sharp, wave-making power woman." He rotated his hips and her head went back at the friction on the aching bundle at her core. "Tonight I want my wife."

Amalia nodded, speech rendered impossible by the man kissing her with a drugging passion. Large hands moved up her calf, up her knee, her quivering thighs and reached her ready heat. "What is it that you want, *ya habibiti*?" he whispered against her forehead.

"You, Zayn. Always you," she managed between blistering breaths and had the reward of seeing the dazzlingly wicked smile of the man she loved, before he entered her and they danced that age-old dance of love again.

* * * * *

The BRIDES FOR BILLIONAIRES *series*
concludes with
MARRIED FOR THE GREEK'S CONVENIENCE
Available January 2017

If you enjoyed this story, don't miss these
other great reads from Tara Pammi
THE UNWANTED CONTI BRIDE
THE SURPRISE CONTI CHILD
THE SHEIKH'S PREGNANT PRISONER
BOUGHT FOR HER INNOCENCE
Available now!

MILLS & BOON®

EXCLUSIVE EXTRACT

Hotel magnate Nate Brunswick's faith in marriage
has been destroyed by his father – but searching
for his beloved grandfather's lost ring leads the
illegitimate Di Sione to an inconvenient engagement!
Mina Mastrantino can only pass the ring on once
she's married. A divorce should be easy…
but their exquisite wedding night gives them
both far more than they planned!

Read on for a sneak preview of
A DEAL FOR THE DI SIONE RING
by Jennifer Hayward

"You're an honorable man, Nate Brunswick. *Grazie.*"

"Not so honorable, Mina." A dark glitter entered his
eyes. "You called me improper not so long ago. I can
be that and more. I am a hard, ruthless businessman who
does what it takes to make money. I will turn a hotel
over in the flash of an eye if I don't see the flesh on the
bones I envisioned when I bought it. I will enjoy a
woman one night and send her packing the next when
I get bored of her company. Know what you're getting
into with me if you accept this. You will learn the
dog-eat-dog approach to life, *not* the civilized one."

Why did something that was intended to be a warning
send a curious shudder through her? Mina drew the wrap
closer around her shoulders, her gaze tangling with
Nate's. The glitter in his eyes stoked to a hot, velvet

shimmer as he took a step forward and ran a finger along the line of her jaw. "Rule number one of this new arrangement, should you so choose to accept it, is to not look at me like that, *wife*. If we do this, we keep things strictly business so both of us walk away after the year with exactly what we want."

Her gaze fell away from his, her blood hot and thick in her veins. "You're misinterpreting me."

"No, I'm not." He brought his mouth to her ear, his warm breath caressing her cheek. "I have a hell of a lot more experience than you do, Mina. I can recognize the signs. They were loud and clear in my hotel room that day and they're loud and clear now."

She took a deep, shuddering breath. To protest further would be futile when her skin felt like it was on fire, her knees like jelly. He watched her like a cat played with a mouse, all powerful and utterly sure of himself. "The only thing that would be more of a disaster than this day's already been," he drawled finally, apparently ready to have mercy on her, "would be for us to end up in bed together. So a partnership it is, Mina." He lifted his glass. "What do you say?"

Don't miss
A DEAL FOR THE DI SIONE RING
by Jennifer Hayward

Available January 2017
www.millsandboon.co.uk

MILLS & BOON®

Why shop at millsandboon.co.uk?

Each year, thousands of romance readers find their perfect read at millsandboon.co.uk. That's because we're passionate about bringing you the very best romantic fiction. Here are some of the advantages of shopping at www.millsandboon.co.uk:

* **Get new books first**—you'll be able to buy your favourite books one month before they hit the shops

* **Get exclusive discounts**—you'll also be able to buy our specially created monthly collections, with up to 50% off the RRP

* **Find your favourite authors**—latest news, interviews and new releases for all your favourite authors and series on our website, plus ideas for what to try next

* **Join in**—once you've bought your favourite books, don't forget to register with us to rate, review and join in the discussions

Visit **www.millsandboon.co.uk**
for all this and more today!

MILLS_WEB